Mary Anne and the Great Romance

Look for these and other books
in the Baby-sitters Club series:

1 Kristy's Great Idea

2 Claudia and the
Phantom Phone Calls

3 The Truth About Stacey

4 Mary Anne Saves the Day

5 Dawn and the
Impossible Three

6 Kristy's Big Day

7 Claudia and Mean Janine

8 Boy-Crazy Stacey

9 The Ghost at Dawn's House

#10 Logan Likes Mary Anne!

#11 Kristy and the Snobs

#12 Claudia and the New Girl

#13 Good-bye Stacey, Good-bye

#14 Hello, Mallory

#15 Little Miss Stoneybrook
. . . and Dawn

#16 Jessi's Secret Language

#17 Mary Anne's
Bad-Luck Mystery

#18 Stacey's Mistake

#19 Claudia and the Bad Joke

#20 Kristy and the
Walking Disaster

#21 Mallory and the
Trouble with Twins

#22 Jessi Ramsey, Pet-sitter

#23 Dawn on the Coast

#24 Kristy and the
Mother's Day Surprise

#25 Mary Anne and the
Search for Tigger

#26 Claudia and the
Sad Good-bye

#27 Jessi and the Superbrat

#28 Welcome Back, Stacey!

#29 Mallory and the
Mystery Diary

#30 Mary Anne and the
Great Romance

#31 Dawn's Wicked Stepsister

Super Specials:
1 Baby-sitters on Board!
2 Baby-sitters'
Summer Vacation
3 Baby-sitters'
Winter Vacation

Mary Anne and the Great Romance

Ann M. Martin

AN
APPLE
PAPERBACK

SCHOLASTIC INC.
New York Toronto London Auckland Sydney

For IRS

Cover art by Hodges Soileau

ISBN 0-590-42498-X

12 11 10 9 8 7 6 5 4 3 2 1   0 1 2 3 4 5/9

Printed in the U.S.A.

First Scholastic printing, January 1990

CHAPTER 1

"Honestly, sometimes living with my mother is like living with a very tall child," said Dawn, and I giggled.

Dawn Schafer is one of my two best friends, and we were spending the evening together because our parents had gone out. What Dawn meant about her mother was that Mrs. Schafer is absentminded and scatterbrained. It's okay for me to say that because Dawn says it all the time.

She said it again now. "Mom is so *scatter*-brained!" (Dawn had just found a high heel in the vegetable drawer of the refrigerator.) She removed it, set it gently on the floor, and said to the shoe, "I hope you thaw out okay." Then she turned to me. "Well? What do you want for dinner? I mean, besides shoes. Mom left a tofu casserole in the fridge — I'm surprised she didn't leave it in her closet — but

I have a feeling you won't want that."

"Do you have any peanut butter?" I asked hopefully.

"Yes, but it's all natural, with no sugar or salt."

"I'll take it." That was better than tofu.

I made myself a peanut butter-and-honey sandwich while Dawn made herself a salad.

We were getting used to these evenings. Our parents weren't just out. They were out *together*, on a *date*. That had been happening more and more lately.

I guess I should stop and explain who Dawn and I are before I tell you any more about our evening. Okay. Besides being best friends, we live in Stoneybrook, Connecticut, and we're both thirteen years old and in eighth grade. My name is Mary Anne Spier. I've lived in Stoneybrook all my life, in the same house, but Dawn moved here in the middle of seventh grade. She moved because her parents got divorced — and she moved all the way from California! She came with her mom and her younger brother, Jeff. The reason they chose to live in Stoneybrook was that Mrs. Schafer grew up here.

One really sad thing (I mean, apart from the

divorce and the move), was that Jeff was never happy here. He couldn't adjust to Connecticut, and he missed California and his dad too much. So after awhile, he moved back there to live with Mr. Schafer. Dawn misses the California half of her family a lot, but she talks to them on the phone pretty often and seems happy in Connecticut now.

Anyway, so Dawn was living here with her mom and no dad, and I'd been living here with my dad and no mom (my mother died when I was really little), and one day the most amazing thing happened. When Dawn was unpacking the stuff her family had moved to Connecticut (and, as you can imagine, this took forever, since Mrs. Schafer wasn't much help), she came across her mother's high school yearbook. It was from her senior year, so of course she looked up her mom's picture. Then she looked up my dad's picture, since we knew they'd gone to school together. And guess what we found out. Our parents had been in love years and years ago!

But *their* parents — well, Dawn's grandparents — didn't approve of the relationship. See, the Porters (Dawn's mom's name used to be Sharon Porter) were quite wealthy. And the

Spiers were not, although — fake out — Dad put himself through law school and became pretty successful.

Anyway, the Porters encouraged Dawn's mother to go to college in California (as far away as she could get from Dad), and my father and Dawn's mom finally went their separate ways. They each got married, and I think they even forgot about each other — sort of.

Then Dawn and I reintroduced them and they began seeing each other again. At first they took things really slowly. Dad is this reserved, somewhat shy man who hadn't dated in years (not since he and my mother had dated), and he didn't want to rush into anything. Dawn's mom didn't want to rush into anything, either. But she *loved* dating again. She's very outgoing. For the longest time she went out with this awful, preppy guy whose nickname was Trip, and whom Dawn and Jeff hated and called the Trip-Man. She went out with some other men, too. (That was because after she got a job, people at work kept fixing her up with their single friends.)

All along, though, she and Dad would see each other from time to time, but now they're the *only* people they date. And they go out a *lot*. That's why Dawn and I were so used to

4

these evenings together. In fact, we weren't just used to them, we *liked* them!

"Let's eat on trays in front of the TV," suggested Dawn. "You know what's on cable tonight?"

"What?" I asked. I had no idea. We don't get cable.

"A Hayley Mills festival."

Dawn just loves this kid who was an actress back in the sixties. Actually, I kind of like her, too. My favorite Hayley Mills movie is *Pollyanna*. Dawn's is *The Parent Trap*.

"A Hayley Mills festival?" I repeated.

"Yup," said Dawn jubilantly. "They're going to show *Pollyanna*, *That Darn Cat*, *The Parent Trap*, and *The Moon-Spinners*."

"That'll take hours!" I cried.

"I know," replied Dawn. "I figure a good ten, if you count commercials and cable-TV ads."

"When does the festival start?" I asked.

"Right now! So let's get our trays."

This is one thing I love about Dawn's house. You can eat in places other than the kitchen and the dining room. At my house there are a lot of rules. Dad used to have even more. He used to be *really strict*, but as I've grown up, he's loosened up. However, I would never

5

be allowed to eat dinner on a tray in front of the TV.

So I carried my sandwich and a banana into the den, and Dawn carried this bean sprout-and-chickpea salad into the den, and we sat down to eat and to get our fill of Hayley Mills. After about an hour, though, we'd *had* our fill. The first movie shown was *Pollyanna*, and although we both like it, we'd seen it recently.

"I guess there really is something to that saying about too much of a good thing," said Dawn.

I nodded. "Yeah. Let's do something else."

First we cleaned up our mess from dinner. (We didn't really need to, since Mrs. Schafer never notices messes, but we always feel we ought to.) Then we went upstairs to Dawn's room.

Here's an interesting thing about her room. In one wall is the entrance to a *secret passage*.

You want to know the truth? That secret passage scares me to death.

You push this place on the molding that decorates the wall, and a panel swings open. If you walk through, you find yourself in a dark, dank passage that leads down a flight of stairs, goes underground below the Schafers' backyard, and eventually comes up through a trapdoor in the floor of their barn.

I guess I should explain here that Dawn's house is really old. It's a farmhouse, and it was built in *1795*. A lot of people have lived in her house over the years (and maybe died there), and there's this one particular person, Jared Mullray, whose voice was last heard coming from the secret passage — but who was never seen again. That was years and years ago, and Dawn and I have good reason to believe that Jared's ghost haunts the passage. So naturally the passage terrifies me. That's just the kind of wimpy person I can be.

Dawn loves the passage. (She considers it hers, since one end of it is in her room.) She loves it partly because it was once a stop on the Underground Railroad, which helped slaves from the South escape to freedom in the North. She also loves it because she just plain loves mysteries, especially ghost stories, and it looks like she's got an honest-to-goodness ghost story at her very own house.

Anyway, to get back to that evening in her bedroom, I sat as far from the passage as possible — on the floor near the doorway to her room, so I could make a fast escape in case I heard moaning or something coming from the passage.

Dawn tried to entertain me by telling me about the time in California when she was baby-sitting for a little boy who believed that pets could understand him the way humans could. He would always say things to the dog like, "Here, Buster, have another cookie. They're good for your teeth. They'll keep the tartar away and then you won't get gingivitis. Visits to the vet are quite important, too, you know. And by the way, you better exercise. You don't want to get overweight. Here, try some push-ups."

I was only half listening to Dawn. I kept thinking about my own house and my own room. Since I've lived my entire life in that house, I always feel safe there . . . and safer in my room . . . and safest of all in my bed.

I was particularly glad I did not have the doorway to a secret passage in my room.

I also began to miss Tigger, my kitten. I always miss him when I'm not with him. I miss him when I'm at school, when I'm baby-sitting, when —

Ring, ring.

"Oh, goody! The phone!" exclaimed Dawn. Dawn just loves getting phone calls. She made a dash for the upstairs extension. I followed her.

8

"Hello?" she said. Then, "Jeff! Hi! How are you? . . . Yeah! Really? That's great." (Dawn put her hand over the receiver and said to me, "Jeff joined a basketball team. He's practically the star player.") She returned to her conversation. "What? . . . Oh, Mary Anne's here. . . . Yeah, Mom and her dad are out again. . . . What? . . . Oh, to dinner and a play in Stamford. . . . Yeah."

Dawn talked for awhile longer, and my mind began to wander. I thought of how my life had changed in the last year. The business of Dad dating Mrs. Schafer was major, of course. Then there was the business of Dad letting up on me and becoming less strict. Finally there was another kind of business — the Baby-sitters Club. Maybe that was the most important business of all.

The club consists of seven members — Dawn, me, Stacey McGill, Claudia Kishi, Mallory Pike, Jessi Ramsey, and Kristy Thomas. Kristy is the president of the club and my other best friend.

And wouldn't you know it — just as Dawn was hanging up with Jeff, and I was thinking of Kristy, the phone rang again. Guess who it was?

Kristy!

She was calling to see if Dawn and I were together and what we were up to. She was baby-sitting that night, the kids were already in bed, and she sounded sort of lonely.

I began to think back to when Kristy and I used to be each other's only best friends. . . .

CHAPTER 2

Up until last summer, for as long as I could remember, Kristy and I had lived next door to each other on Bradford Court. (Claudia Kishi lives across the street.) Kristy and I were nearly inseparable, even though we are opposites in terms of personality. But we were the best of friends anyway. We still are — except that a few things have changed. One, Dawn moved here and she became my other best friend, especially after our parents began going out. Two, Kristy's mother remarried and the Thomases moved across town.

This is beginning to sound a little complicated, so let me back up and tell you about the members of the Baby-sitters Club. As I said, the president of the BSC is Kristy. Like Dawn and me, she's thirteen and in eighth grade. Unlike Dawn and me, she has a very unusual family. Kristy has three brothers —

Sam and Charlie, who are in high school, and David Michael, who's only seven. When David Michael was quite little, Mr. Thomas walked out on the family and never came back. So Mrs. Thomas just took things in hand and raised her four kids alone, getting a really good job at a big company in Stamford, Connecticut. Then, when Kristy was in seventh grade, Mrs. Thomas started going out with this man named Watson Brewer, who is an actual millionaire. They finally got married, even though Kristy didn't want them to. She hated the idea of a new father, especially one who was going bald. But Watson has two adorable children — Karen, who's six, and Andrew, who's four — and slowly she reconciled herself to the idea of the wedding and of moving into Watson's mansion. Now I, personally, would have died to live in a mansion, but believe me, I could also understand about not wanting to leave the house you've grown up in. Anyway, it's a good thing Kristy *did* move to a mansion because her family is so big now. Living there are her brothers; her stepfather, Watson; her mom; and every other weekend, Andrew and Karen. Plus, her family recently adopted Emily, a little girl from Vietnam, and when *that* happened, Nannie, her grandmother, moved in to help care for Emily, since both Watson and Kristy's mom work.

Here are the important things to know about Kristy: She's a tomboy and coaches a softball team, Kristy's Krushers, for little kids. She's the shortest girl in our class, she's got brown hair and brown eyes, and she's on the immature side. She doesn't care much about the way she looks. She always wears the same kind of outfit: blue jeans, a turtleneck shirt, a sweater (well, not in the summer, of course), and running shoes. Sometimes she wears a baseball cap with a picture of a collie on it. That's because her family used to own this wonderful old collie, Louie, but he got sick and had to be put to sleep. Now they have a Bernese mountain dog named Shannon, plus Watson has this old, fat cat named Boo-Boo.

A few others things about Kristy — she has a BIG mouth (she just can't help saying what she's thinking), she gets lots of good ideas (the idea for the Baby-sitters Club was hers), and most important, she's terrific with kids.

Claudia Kishi is the vice-president of the BSC. I always think it's so weird that Claudia, Kristy, and I could have grown up together (right from the time we were born) and have wound up as such different people. Claudia is one of the coolest people I know. She has an artistic flair that extends to her clothing and hair and just generally the way she looks. What I mean is that Claud is a terrific artist — she can paint, draw, sculpt, make collages, you name it — and those talents show up in her appearance. She always wears the trendiest outfits. For instance, at our last meeting she was wearing layers — a shocking-pink tunic over a white shirt with pink and yellow umbrellas printed on it. Over the tunic was a wide, low-slung yellow belt with a pink plastic buckle. The shirt, but not the tunic, was tucked into a pair of black knickers, and below the knickers were yellow stockings.

Then there's her hair. Claud's hair is something else. Her family is Japanese-American, and Claud has this shiny, black hair. But her hair isn't just shiny and dark, it's long. And Claud can find a million ways to wear it. At that last meeting, she had divided it into five braids and had woven pink and yellow ribbons into the braids. Claud also has dark, almond-shaped eyes and a super-creamy complexion.

She is so cool.

Claud lives with her parents and her older sister, Janine, who is a true genius. Janine is so smart that even though she's only in high school she takes classes at the local community college. Claudia's grandmother, Mimi, who was a very special person, used to live with her family, but Mimi died not long ago. That was really sad.

Here's what Claud likes: art, junk food, and Nancy Drew mysteries. Her room is a real mess because she's got art supplies scattered everywhere. And since her parents don't approve of either Claud's junk-food habit or Nancy Drew, she has to stash those books and the food where they won't be found. She's got mysteries under her mattress and candy in her desk drawers. Here's what Claud doesn't like: school. She's very smart, but her teachers are always saying that she doesn't apply herself. Mr. and Mrs. Kishi finally had to tell Claud that the only way she could stay in the BSC was if she kept her grades up to at least a C average. So far, she has.

I'm the secretary of the club, and I guess you already know pretty much about me. I'm on the shy side, my dad dates Dawn's mom, I live with my father and Tigger, and Dawn and Kristy are my best friends. I lost my mother when I was very little, and I've grown up in the house I was born in.

Here are some things you don't know about

me yet: I actually *look* a little like Kristy. I've got brown hair and brown eyes, too, and I used to be on the short side, but now I'm growing. I'm a couple of inches taller than Kristy. Also, until recently I didn't care much about the way I looked. Well, that's not true. The fact of the matter is that Dad used to pick out my clothes for me and I always ended up looking like a baby in these dumb jumpers or plaid kilts. But when he loosened up, he let me pick out my own clothes. I'm nowhere near as cool as Claudia, but I did buy some neat stuff. If Claud's fashion sense could be rated a ten, and Kristy's a two, I guess I must be about a six. Maybe a seven.

Another thing about me: I am very sensitive. This is good and bad. It's good because I think it makes me more understanding of other people. My friends in the BSC often come to me when they have problems because they know I'll listen and be sympathetic and sometimes offer advice, but I try not to judge them — just to understand them. Being sensitive is bad because I cry at the least little thing. I'm incredibly sentimental. Maybe being sentimental is why I'm the only one in the club to have . . . a boyfriend! Can you believe it? *I* barely can. His name is Logan Bruno and he comes from the South — Louisville, Kentucky. He's actually part of our club, but I'll have to explain that later.

Enough about me.

On to Stacey McGill, the treasurer of the club. Stacey is originally from New York City, and is about as cool and sophisticated as Claudia. Maybe that's why Stacey and Claud are best friends. (Guess what Stacey's real name is. Anastasia Elizabeth!) If Claudia's fashion rating is a ten, then Stacey's must be a nine and a half. Her clothes are amazing, too, but she doesn't have that artistic flair that Claud does. (Did I mention that Claudia often makes her own jewelry? She makes ceramic beads or earrings, or beaded bracelets, things like that.) Stacey has no interest in art, but she does have a body wave in her short blonde hair, and pierced ears. (In case you're wondering, Claudia has one hole in one ear and *two* in the other; Stacey, Mallory, and Jessi have regular pierced ears; Dawn has two holes in *each* ear, and Kristy and I plan never, ever to let someone punch holes through our earlobes. The very idea makes me shiver.)

Anyway, Stacey has had an interesting, but sort of tough life. For starters, she has diabetes, which is a disease in which her body doesn't make the right amount of insulin to control the level of sugar in her blood. That might not sound serious but it *can* be *very* serious. Stacey has to give herself injections of insulin every day and stick to a controlled diet. I mean, she can only eat certain foods (NO sweets) at certain times, and she has to take in a certain number of calories every day no matter what. She also has to go to the doctor pretty often and check her urine every day. That's gross, but it has to be done. If Stacey doesn't do all these things, she could wind up in a coma.

Plus, Stacey was born in New York. She lived there until the beginning of seventh grade. Then the company her father works for transferred him to their Connecticut branch, so the McGills moved to Stoneybrook. That was when we all got to know Stacey. But the McGills had only been here about a year when the company transferred Mr. McGill *back* to New York. What a drag. We missed Stacey a lot, especially Claudia. However, the McGills had been in the city again for only a little while when Stacey's parents decided to get a divorce. Then the worst possible thing (for Stacey) happened. Her father stayed in New York (because of his job), but her mother bought a house back here in Stoneybrook. So Stacey had to choose where to live. Her parents said the decision was hers. Boy, was that a tough one. Stacey didn't want to hurt either her mother or her father, plus she likes both New York City and Stoneybrook. In the end, she moved back to Connecticut with her mom — but she visits her dad a *lot*.

Stacey doesn't have any brothers or sisters or pets. She is very close to her mother, however.

Okay, now it's Dawn's turn. She's the alternate officer of our club. (More about that later.) Again, you already know a few things about Dawn. Her parents are divorced, too, her dad and brother live in California, her mother's parents live here in Stoneybrook, Mrs. Schafer (or maybe I should say the scatterbrained Mrs. Schafer) is dating my dad, Dawn is one of my best friends, and she lives in an old farmhouse with a secret passage.

Here's what Dawn looks like: she has the longest, palest hair you can imagine. It's smooth as silk and almost the color of milk. Her eyes are a bright blue, and she's of average height and on the thin side. One thing I like a lot about Dawn is that she's a real individual. She dresses however she pleases (my friends and I think of her style as California casual), she eats health food and no meat while the rest of us (well, except for Stacey) are cramming ourselves with junk food, and she stands up for what she believes in. She hardly ever lets other people get her down. Dawn visits her dad and Jeff when she can, but I know she misses them. Personally, I think she could do with a pet.

The last two members of the BSC, the junior officers, are Jessica Ramsey (Jessi for short) and Mallory Pike (Mal for short). While Dawn, Kristy, Stacey, Claud, and I are eighth-graders, Mal and Jessi are sixth-graders. They're eleven years old. They're also best friends. And like most best friends, they're alike in many ways, and different in many ways. They're alike in that neither of them has divorced parents and they're both the oldest in their families. It's tough being the oldest, I think, and Mal and Jessi want to grow up a lot faster than their parents want them to — although they *were* allowed to have their ears pierced recently, so that was a good sign. They both love to read, too, especially horse stories. I think their favorite author is Marguerite Henry, who wrote *Misty of Chincoteague* and *Stormy, Misty's Foal*, but they like Barbara Morgenroth (she wrote *Impossible Charlie*) and another author named Lynn Hall, too.

Each of their families has a pet hamster.

The differences between Mal and Jessi are, first of all, that Mal is white and Jessi is black. Second, Mal had to get braces. Then there are their families. Mallory's is huge. She has *seven* younger brothers and sisters, including a set of identical triplets — boys. Jessi's family is average sized. She has an eight-year-old sister named Rebecca (Becca for short), and a baby brother with a funny nickname. His real name is John Philip Ramsey, Jr., but when he was born, he was the tiniest baby in the hospital, so the nurses called him Squirt. Even though he's caught up to other babies his age by now (he's sort of walking), the Ramseys still call him Squirt.

Also, while both Jessi and Mal like to read (and, I might add, make endless gum chains), Jessi wants to be a professional ballet dancer one day, and Mal wants to be a writer and illustrator of children's books. They're both very talented. You should read some of Mal's stories. And you should see Jessi dance. She takes lessons at a special school and has performed on stage in front of hundreds of people.

One final difference between the girls: Mal grew up in Stoneybrook, and Jessi's family moved here from New Jersey not long ago. There are very few blacks in Stoneybrook, which has been hard on Jessi, but she's adjusting. And so are some of the people who originally gave the Ramseys a hard time.

So there you have it. Those are the members of the BSC. Now you know all about Kristy and Dawn and me and the rest of us.

I stopped daydreaming. Dawn handed me the phone and I talked to Kristy for fifteen minutes. By the time we hung up, I could tell she felt better.

Good. I'm one of her best friends, and what are best friends for?

CHAPTER 3

"Okay! I'm here! The meeting can start now!"

Kristy Thomas never just arrives — she makes an entrance.

It was a Baby-sitters Club meeting day and Kristy was the last to arrive. You'd think she'd always be the first, and I'm sure she'd like to be, but since she moved across town, she depends on Charlie, her oldest brother, to drop her off at our meetings and pick her up later. (We pay him for this service.)

Our meetings are held in Claudia's bedroom because she's the only one of us with her own phone and personal phone number. This is important to us, because otherwise, we'd have to rely on some grown-up's phone, and I know we'd always worry about tying it up, or else we'd have to wait while the grown-up was on the phone, and then our clients would call us and get a busy signal.

Confused? I guess I better explain how our club works. See, three afternoons a week (Mondays, Wednesdays, and Fridays) we meet from five-thirty until six o'clock. Our clients know we meet then, and they call us when they need a baby-sitter. Then I check our record book to see which one of us is free, and we call the client back to tell her (or him) who the sitter will be. That's the beauty of the club. With seven possible sitters, someone is bound to be available, so our clients are never disappointed.

How do our clients know when we meet? Because we advertise, that's how. We send out fliers. When we first started the club, we even placed an ad in the local paper. By now, we've got a reputation as responsible, reliable, fun baby-sitters, so news of our club also spreads by word of mouth.

As you know by reading this far, each of us has a special job in the club. Kristy is our president because she's the one who came up with the idea for the club in the first place. Back at the beginning of seventh grade, she and her older brothers were responsible for taking care of David Michael after school or any evening when their mother was busy. But there came a time when Kristy's mom (I never know whether to call her Mrs. Thomas or Mrs. Brewer now) needed a sitter and neither Kristy nor her brothers were free. So Mrs. Thomas (that was her name then) got on the phone to try to find a baby-sitter. Kristy watched her make call after call without any luck — and that was when her great idea was born. Wouldn't it be terrific, she thought, if her mom could dial one number and reach a whole bunch of eager sitters? So she got together with Claudia, Stacey, and me and we started the Baby-sitters Club. It caught on quickly, and when Dawn moved here, we asked her to join, because we had so many clients. Then the club grew even more, and Stacey moved *away*, so we replaced her with both Jessi and Mal. But, of course, when Stacey returned, we let her right back in the club.

Anyway, Kristy's main responsibilities are to run the meetings and to keep thinking up good ideas — like Kid-Kits. Kid-Kits are boxes (we each made one) that we decorated and then filled with a few of our old games, toys, and books, and new items like coloring books or stickers or crayons. Then we sometimes take the Kid-Kits with us on a sitting job. Our charges love them. There's just something intriguing (to a little kid) about toys that aren't your own. And Kristy seemed to know that. That's one reason she's such a good club president — even if she can be too bossy. She also makes us keep a club notebook in which we have to write up every job we go on. Most of us don't like doing this, but we have to admit that it's helpful to see how our friends handle baby-sitting problems, and to know what's going on at the homes of the people we sit for.

Claudia is our vice-president, mostly because we use her room as our club headquarters and tie up her phone three times a week.

As secretary, my job is to keep the record book (not to be confused with the notebook) in order and up-to-date. The record book is where we record all important club information, such as our clients' names, addresses and phone numbers, and information about the children. Probably the most important pages in the book are the appointment pages. That's where I keep track of everyone's schedules — Jessi's dance classes, Mal's orthodontist appointments, Claud's art lessons, etc. — as well as our baby-sitting jobs. When a call comes in, it's up to me to check the schedule, see who's free for the job, and help decide who should take it if more than one person is available. It is a very important job and I am proud that I have never once made a scheduling mistake.

Stacey, the treasurer, has the job of collecting our club dues each week. *No one* likes to part with her money, even though it goes toward good things — new items for the Kid-Kits, Claud's monthly phone bills, Charlie's fee to drive Kristy to the meetings, and fun things such as club slumber parties. Stacey also records the money we earn on jobs (she does this in the record book), but this is just for our own information. We don't divide up the money. Each of us gets to keep whatever we make.

Stacey is practically a genius at math.

As I said, Dawn is the club's alternate officer. That means that she gets to take on the job of any officer who can't make a meeting for some reason. (She's dying to be the president one day, but Kristy has never missed a meeting.) When Stacey went back to New York for that year, Dawn became the treasurer, but she happily took over her old job when Stacey returned. Dawn doesn't care much about math and numbers, even if the numbers represent money. She's a very good alternate officer and, like the rest of us, she's a good baby-sitter, too.

Jessi and Mal, our junior officers, don't have actual jobs. *Junior officer* means that they're not allowed to baby-sit at night yet, unless they're taking care of their own brothers and sisters. But they're a great help to us because they can handle lots of the afternoon and weekend jobs, which frees us older sitters up for evening jobs.

Even so, there are times when calls come in for jobs that, for one reason or another, none of us can handle. When that happens, we call on our associate members. There are two of them. They don't come to meetings, but they're responsible baby-sitters who can back us up so that we don't have to disappoint any of our clients by telling them that we can't provide them with a sitter. One of the associate members is a friend of Kristy's in her new neighborhood, Shannon Kilbourne. Guess who the other associate member is — Logan Bruno!

I guess that's really all you need to know about our club. As you can see, Kristy has planned it well and keeps it running smoothly.

As soon as Kristy had dashed into club headquarters, she plopped down in Claud's director's chair (that's where she always sits), exchanged her collie cap for her president's visor, and stuck a pencil over her ear.

"Are we all here?" she asked. "Oh, no. We're not. Dawn's missing."

It was only 5:25. Kristy is a stickler for starting meetings on time. That's both good and bad. It's good because it's responsible and because you always know you have exactly until 5:30 to get to Claudia's room. Kristy won't start a meeting early. On the other hand, she won't start a meeting a second late, which is the bad part. As soon as Claudia's digital clock, our official timepiece, turns to five-thirty — *boom*, the meeting starts, whether you're there or not. And if you come in late, Kristy usually isn't happy, although she won't be mean to you or anything, unless it's, like, the fifth time in a row that you've been late.

We waited for Dawn. Kristy sat in her chair, reading through the club notebook.

Stacey was perched backward in Claud's desk chair, facing into the room, her arms resting on the top rung. She was examining her nail polish, which was pale pink with iridescent sparkles in it.

"I'll have to redo my nails," she was saying. "Three of them are chipped."

"I don't know why you bother with polish," I said. "It's such a pain. You have to worry about it all the time."

"I know," replied Stace, "but it makes my hands look great!"

Claudia and I were sitting on her bed, leaning against her wall. (When Dawn arrived, we'd move over to make room for her.) Claud's leg was propped up on a pillow. She broke it awhile back and in certain weather, usually before it rains, her leg hurts her a lot. The doctor said it might always do that.

Claudia has a good attitude about it. "I'm probably more accurate than that weather forecaster on Channel Four," she's always saying.

Claud shifted uncomfortably on the bed. "Anyone hungry?" she asked.

Since it was nearly dinnertime, we all were.

"There are some M and Ms in a box under my bed, and a package of crackers under the desk," she told us.

"We'll get them!" said Jessi and Mal at the same time. They were sitting on the floor and were within easy reach of the food and didn't want Claud to have to get up.

Jessi scrambled for the crackers and Mal peered under the bed.

"Which box?" Mal asked, and sneezed, adding, "It's dusty under here!"

"Sorry," said Claud. "Um, the M and Ms are in the woodcut supplies box — I think."

Mal found a box labeled WODCUT SUPPLISE. (What did I tell you about Claudia's schoolwork? She couldn't spell properly if someone offered her a million dollars.) Mal opened the box, pulled out a new bag of plain M&Ms, and passed them around.

Everyone took some except Stacey.

"The crackers are for you," Claud told her.

"Thanks, but I can't have them. The doctor wants me to be stricter than usual about snacks. I can't eat until dinner. Dawn'll want them, though."

Stacey was right. When Dawn blew in at 5:29, she made a grab for the crackers. "I'm *starving*," she announced.

And then Kristy got the meeting underway. We took care of club business and waited for calls to start coming in. The first one came precisely at 5:35. The next one was at 5:38. We, (well, *I*) became very busy scheduling jobs while the others took turns answering the phone.

At 5:51 came a call that Mallory answered.

"Hello, Baby-sitters Club," she said. There

31

was a pause. Then, "Hi, Mrs. Arnold! How are you?"

Mrs. Arnold is the mother of identical twins, Marilyn and Carolyn. Mal had once had a steady but short-term job with the twins while their mother took on a fundraising project for Stoneybrook Elementary School. The twins had started out as terrors, but wound up as very different little girls — much sweeter and nicer once people began to see that they were individuals, not two of a kind. Anyway, now Mrs. Arnold was working on another school project and would need a regular sitter for several weeks. We couldn't provide her with *one* regular sitter, but we did manage to get her a sitter for every afternoon when she would need one. Guess who got most of the jobs? Me!

"Hmm," said Mallory thoughtfully when she'd hung up the phone. "I wonder what the twins are like now. We haven't sat for them much lately."

If only we had. I might have been a little better prepared for what was to come.

CHAPTER 4

*D*ing-dong.

I rang the Arnolds' bell and waited for the sound of four feet running to the door. Marilyn and Carolyn used to hate baby-sitters because nobody, including sitters, could tell the twins apart. But since the girls are different now, they like sitters.

However, only one pair of feet dashed to the door. Marilyn's. As soon as she opened it, I recognized her. Here's why. Up until the girls were eight years old, their parents were so thrilled with the idea of identical twins that they insisted on dressing Marilyn and Carolyn in exactly the same outfits every day, right down to their jewelry. And their hair was styled the same way. Furthermore, they were given the same toys. And they still share a room with identical furniture on either side. Carolyn's half of the room looks like a mirror image of Marilyn's half. It used to be that the only difference between the girls is that Marilyn takes piano lessons (Carolyn is tone deaf), while Carolyn likes science.

Those two things haven't changed, but a lot of others sure have. When Mallory was sitting for the twins she saw how miserable they were. The kids at school couldn't tell them apart, so they called *both* of them "Marilyn-or-Carolyn." Even Mallory couldn't tell them apart unless they wore their name bracelets. What no one knew (because the girls just weren't mature enough to figure out how to tell their parents) was that Marilyn and Carolyn desperately wanted their own, personal, separate identities. Marilyn wanted to grow her hair out. Carolyn wanted hers cut. Neither one liked the frilly clothes their parents chose for them. Marilyn wanted simpler clothes, Carolyn wanted trendier clothes. Furthermore, Marilyn was the more dominant twin. She's kind of like Kristy. But Carolyn was more outgoing — like Claudia or Stacey.

They were two different seven-year-olds when Mallory first met them — only no one knew it. Not, that is, until Mallory started talking to the twins and finally came to understand them. Then she found the nerve to help them have a discussion with their mother and even convince Mrs. Arnold to let them spend their birthday money (they turned eight recently) on new clothes. New *nonidentical* clothes. Later, Carolyn got her hair cut short — *very* stylishly, with longer curls down the back of her neck — and now Marilyn's hair has grown out an inch or two.

So when a girl with longish hair, wearing a simple gray skirt, a white blouse, white kneesocks, and red shoes opened the door, I knew right away that it was Marilyn.

"Hi!" I said.

"Hi!" she replied. She was trying to sound happy, but I could tell that something was bothering her.

I stepped into the Arnolds' front hall. "Where's Carolyn?" I asked.

"Out."

"Out? Out where?"

"With her friends."

Obviously, this was a touchy subject, so I didn't pursue it. Anyway, Mrs. Arnold came bustling in from the living room then. Somehow when she's around, the calmest situation can turn into a flurry of excitement.

"Hello, Mary Anne," she greeted me. "Oh, you brought your Kid-Kit. Great. Now, Marilyn's the only one here. Carolyn's off with her friends. She's over at Haley Braddock's. There was a chance she and Haley are going to visit Vanessa Pike, so if you need Carolyn, try one of those places." (I noticed Marilyn scowling then, but Mrs. Arnold didn't see it.) "I'll be at Stoneybrook Elementary," Mrs. Arnold went on. "The number for the school office is posted by the phone. Mr. Arnold's office number is there, too, along with the emergency numbers. I should be back in about two hours. Maybe two and a half. Marilyn, you have fun with Mary Anne. And if Carolyn comes home, *be nice to her*," she added ominously.

"Okay," said Marilyn sulkily.

Mrs. Arnold left then, and I said brightly to Marilyn, "You know, you can go play with Carolyn, if you want. I won't mind."

Marilyn looked sad. "You don't want to play with me, either?" she said.

Oops. What did Marilyn mean? "Of course I want to play with you," I assured her. "I brought the Kid-Kit with me, didn't I?"

Marilyn nodded.

"I just thought you might want to play with your sister and your friends," I added. "I'd come with you."

"Nah," said Marilyn. "They're not my

friends. I don't have any. I mean, I have a —
a different friend."

"Oh. Well, that's nice. What's her name?"

"Her name is . . . Gozzie Kunka."

"Gozzie Kunka!" I exclaimed. "What kind
of name is that?"

"Foreign. She comes from a faraway place,"
replied Marilyn. "She's new at school," she
went on. "She's not in my grade, but I met
her on the playground. She didn't have anyone to play with or talk to, so I sat down next
to her on the swings."

"Does she speak English?" I asked.

Marilyn and I had moved into the living
room and were opening the Kid-Kit.

"Oh, yes. Very well. She just has a sort of —
what do you call it?"

"An accent?" I suggested.

"Yeah, an accent. But I can understand
her."

Marilyn took a puzzle out of the Kid-Kit,
but she didn't dump it out. Instead she said,
"You know what Gozzie told me? She told me
that she can ride a horse bareback. And that
once when she and her family were in Paris,
they ate snails and frogs' legs."

"Ew," I said.

"I know. That's what I said, too. But Gozzie

37

said the frogs' legs were good — kind of like chicken. She didn't like the snails, though. They were rubbery and covered with garlic. . . . You know what else Gozzie has eaten?"

"What?" I asked.

"Sushi, elk meat, and rice paper. She has traveled everywhere."

"She sounds fascinating."

"Oh, she is." I thought Marilyn would dump the puzzle out then, but instead she said, "Once Gozzie and her family were on a plane, and a man said he was going to hijack it. It turned out he was only fooling, but he got arrested anyway. The plane made an emergency landing in Brazil and a whole bunch of police officers trooped onto the plane and arrested him. They had to carry him out because he made a fuss and wouldn't walk."

"Gosh," I said, "that must have been awfully scary."

"It was. Gozzie's family was too upset even to eat the meals on the plane trip." Marilyn finally spread the puzzle pieces on the floor and began fitting them together, but while she did, she kept talking.

"Carolyn has gotten to be an awful pain. She spends all her time with Haley and Vanessa and some other girls around here. Haley and Vanessa aren't even in our grade. They're a whole year older."

"Sometimes that doesn't matter," I told her. "I'm friends with Mallory Pike and Jessi Ramsey and I'm *two* years older than they are."

Marilyn shrugged. She worked on the puzzle for awhile. Then she read to me from *Pippi Longstocking*. We were in the middle of a chapter about a very funny tea party when Carolyn came home.

"Hi, Mary Anne!" she cried.

"Hi, yourself," I said. "You look terrific."

Carolyn, with her snazzy haircut and in her equally snazzy clothes, grinned broadly.

Marilyn scowled.

Then Carolyn said, "Me and Haley and Vanessa and maybe Charlotte Johanssen are thinking of forming a club. A club for girls. We will only let certain people be in it."

"Certain snobs," I heard Marilyn mutter.

Carolyn heard her, too. "You take that back!" she cried. "My friends are not snobs. They're very nice. They're just . . . cool," she added tauntingly.

"They're jerks," Marilyn said, and stomped up to her room.

I let her stay there for ten minutes. Then I went upstairs to make sure she was okay. I found her lying on her bed in her half of the identical room. She was just staring at the ceiling.

"Why don't you come back down?" I asked her. "I've got new crayons in the Kid-Kit. And a new pad of paper. You and Carolyn could make some pictures for your mom and dad."

Reluctantly, Marilyn followed me. Then she and Carolyn sat at the kitchen table and colored. But not in a friendly way. They never spoke, except to say things like, "Daddy says *I'm* the best artist." Or, "Who cares if Daddy will like your old picture better?"

Hmm. What had gone wrong? I wondered. I'd thought the twins would be happier once they were allowed to be individuals. But these were two very angry little girls.

CHAPTER 5

I left the Arnolds' that night feeling disturbed. I was sorry to see the twins so unhappy. But as I walked home, my head cleared. I felt better by the time I reached my house.

The very first thing I did when I unlocked our front door and let myself inside was kiss Tigger.

"Hi, you little Munchkin," I said softly. (Tigger only has about a thousand nicknames.)

Tigger turned on his purr right away. I just love it when he does that. He squinches his eyes closed and looks like the happiest kitten in the universe.

"I bet you're hungry, aren't you?" I said. "Well, so am I. I better start both our dinners."

Starting dinner is my job. Dad usually gets home between six o'clock and six-thirty, and I'm usually home around six. So I get things going. That morning, we had decided to heat up this lasagna that we'd made a few weeks ago and frozen, and to toss a salad to go with it. So, as soon as I'd fed Tigger, I set the oven and then got out the makings for a really super salad: lettuce, carrots, mushrooms, red and green peppers, cucumbers, olives, celery, hard-boiled eggs, and these salty things my father likes called sun-dried tomatoes.

The lasagna was just beginning to make the kitchen smell nice, and a lot of the ingredients for the salad had been chopped up, when Dad came home. He kissed both Tigger and me on the tops of our heads.

"Mmm, I'm starved," he announced.

"Me, too," I replied. I was going to tell him about the Arnold twins when Dad sat down at the kitchen table with this particular look on his face which means he has something to say. So I kept my mouth shut.

"Guess what," Dad began.

"What?" I replied.

"Mrs. Schafer has to work late tonight."

This was news? It was like saying, "Guess what. Tonight it will get dark." Mrs. Schafer works late lots of evenings. She knows she has to work hard if she's going to get anywhere in the company that hired her.

"Um . . . oh," I said.

"Well, I was wondering," Dad went on, "if you'd like to invite Dawn over for dinner. We've got plenty of lasagna, there's no meat in it, and I'll help you make some extra salad."

"Sure!" I replied. I love having Dawn over.

"Great," said Dad. "Go ahead and give her a call."

So I did. And of course Dawn was thrilled with the invitation. Who wants to eat alone? Dad even gave us permission to do our homework together.

By seven o'clock, Dad had picked Dawn up (she could have ridden her bike over, but then she'd have had to ride it home in the dark later), and the three of us were sitting down to dinner.

For some reason, Dad had insisted that we eat in the dining room instead of the kitchen, which is where we almost *always* eat, even when Dawn or my other friends are over. Dad had even lit candles and used our good china.

I was beginning to think that my father had something on his mind.

I was right.

After he'd politely asked us how school had been that day, he put down his fork and cleared his throat. "Ahem, ahem."

Dawn and I glanced at each other, and Dawn raised her eyebrows.

"As you know," my father continued, "Dawn's mother's birthday is coming up." (I didn't know that, but Dawn did, of course.) "And I was thinking that it might be nice to surprise her."

My *father* was suggesting a *surprise* party? He'd die if anyone ever gave *him* one. What had gotten into him?

Dawn smiled but said tactfully, "That's a really nice idea, Mr. Spier, but I don't know how Mom would feel about being surprised."

"Oh, I don't mean anything big," Dad assured us. "I'm not talking about a crowd of people jumping out from behind couches. I was just thinking that the three of us could surprise her with dinner at a restaurant."

"I think she'd like that," said Dawn slowly. "I really do. But how would we surprise her?"

"I'm not sure yet," Dad replied. "Maybe I could ask a client of hers to suggest a business dinner — "

"On the night *before* her birthday," I interrupted.

Dad frowned at me. He can't stand being interrupted.

"Sorry," I said softly.

44

"I could ask a client," Dad repeated, "to suggest a business dinner. If she agrees, then I'll call and make the reservation. We'll show up a few minutes early, so when your mother arrives, Dawn, we'll already be there."

"That's a good plan," said Dawn. "She wouldn't mind a surprise like that."

"We could make the dinner really special, too," I added. "We could bring along her presents and order a cake."

"But no waiters or waitresses singing 'Happy Birthday,'" said Dawn.

"Dad? Could you order a bottle of champagne?" I asked. "I mean, just for you and Mrs. Schafer — Dawn and I wouldn't ask for any. And the waiter could leave it in one of those silver buckets by the table."

"And we could bring her a red rose," said Dawn. "Well, you could, Mr. Spier. She would love it."

Dad was smiling. "I'm certainly glad I consulted you two," he said. (I knew he'd forgiven me for interrupting him.) "You could hire yourselves out as party-planners."

"Hey, good idea!" I said, before I remembered that Dad is not in love with the word "hey."

But all *he* said was, "Don't even think about

it. I was just kidding. You've got enough to do between school and baby-sitting."

I knew he was right.

We talked about Mrs. Schafer's surprise for most of the rest of the meal. One thing seemed odd to me: This birthday wasn't going to be a big one for Mrs. Schafer. I know because I said, "So how old is your mom going to be, Dawn?" (I didn't even look at Dad. I was sure he would have disapproved of the question. Dad is *so* old-fashioned. He still thinks it's rude to ask "a lady" her age.)

"Forty-three," Dawn replied, without blinking an eye.

Hmm. Why was Dad making such a big fuss over a forty-third birthday. Why not wait until her forty-fifth? Oh, well. Maybe he just wanted to do something nice. After all, it would be the first birthday Dawn's mom had celebrated since she and Dad started going out together.

When dinner was over, Dad volunteered to do the dishes so Dawn and I could start our homework. We didn't tell him that we had only a little homework that night. We wanted a chance to talk. So we did our math and science problems in a flash and just hoped we'd gotten the right answers.

As soon as we were finished, I said, "What are you going to give your mom for her birthday?"

Without hesitating, Dawn replied, "A day-planner. You know, one of those fancy books that help you organize your whole life. She really needs one. And she said she wants one."

"Oh. I'm not sure what to get her. Maybe I could get a pen to go with the day-planner. I mean, a nice pen. Not just a Bic or something."

"Nah. She'd lose it."

"Oh. Then how about a book?"

"I don't know. She's pretty picky about what she reads."

I felt sort of hurt. Why couldn't Dawn be helpful? Then I got a terrific idea. Mrs. Schafer loves jewelry. "I know! A nice piece of jewelry!" I cried.

"Great!" exclaimed Dawn.

"Maybe a pin shaped like a cat. I saw a really pretty one in — "

"Forget it. Mom doesn't like cats."

Finally I lost my temper (sort of). "Well, could you give me some help here? You're just shooting down all my ideas."

"I'm sorry. It's just that I know my mother

better than you do, and your ideas aren't —
aren't — "

"Aren't what?" I demanded.

Dawn shrugged. "Mom and I are so *close*,
that's all. I guess it's hard for me to be understanding when someone has the wrong
idea about her."

I jumped off the bed and faced Dawn with
my fists clenched. "I don't have any *wrong*
ideas about her. You make it sound like I think
she's some sleazy old . . . I don't know . . ."

"*Sorry*," said Dawn, not sounding sorry at
all.

I sat down on the bed again, and Tigger
crawled into my lap for comfort. He hates
fights and commotion. Usually he leaves the
room.

Dawn and I were silent for a few moments.
At last Dawn asked how my baby-sitting job
had gone that afternoon. I told her about the
twins and their new friends.

"*Gozzie Kunka?*" Dawn repeated in amazement when I told her about Marilyn's friend.

"That's what she said her name is."

"I've never heard of a name like that."

"Neither have I. But you never know."

Dawn smiled. "For the longest time," she

said, "I thought Logan Bruno was a pretty weird name."

I threw a pillow at Dawn and she threw one back at me. We started giggling and couldn't stop.

Our fight was over.

CHAPTER 6

Tuesday

I sat for Matt and Haley today. I just love those kids. Matt is so neat. Even when he's signing to you, you don't think of him as handicapped or different -- just as a seven-year-old kid. By the way, Matt taught me a new sign today. It's the one for "owl." You put your hands around your eyes to make them look as round as an owl's. Isn't that neat?

Anyway, Carolyn Arnold came over to play with Haley while

50

I was there, and since I knew that Mal was sitting for some of her younger brothers and sisters this afternoon, I took my kids over to her house for what turned out to be a game of Sardines. That was when the fun really began.....

In case you don't know, Matt and Haley Braddock are two of our regular sitting charges. Matt is seven and Haley is nine. They're great kids. The unusual thing about their family, though, is that since Matt is profoundly deaf and doesn't speak, he and Haley and their parents communicate using sign language. All us sitters, especially Jessi, and even some of the kids in the neighborhood, have learned a little about signing. If we couldn't sign, we couldn't "talk" to Matt. (He doesn't read lips. Reading lips is very difficult. Try watching TV sometime and blocking your ears. Then see how much you understand. I'll bet it's hardly anything. The "p" and "b" sounds look exactly the same. So do the "d" and "t" sounds. Plus, try lip-reading someone who's got a mustache. Forget it. You can barely see a thing.)

Anyway, Matt talks with his hands just like most people talk with their mouths. There are signs for tons of words (like "owl," which Jessi learned today). If you don't know the sign for a word, you can spell it, since there are also signs for the letters of the alphabet. When you spell out a word, it's called finger spelling. Matt is the best signer of all of us, since he signs all day long at his special school, but Haley and their parents are almost as good as Matt is, and when we're having trouble communicating with Matt, Haley is our interpreter.

Jessi arrived at the Braddocks' right after school let out. Not long after Mrs. Braddock had left, the doorbell rang. (A light flashed in every room of the house at the same time, so Matt knew the bell had rung, too.) Matt and Haley raced for the door.

"It's Carolyn!" Haley cried, signing at the same time. "I just know it."

"Check before you open the door," Jessi warned Haley.

She checked. It was Carolyn.

Carolyn bounced in, wearing an oversized shirt, tight blue leggings, and flat blue shoes.

"Hi!" she cried.

You'd think she and Haley hadn't just seen each other in school. (Well, they *are* in different grades.)

Jessi gave the kids a snack, and then signed and said, "What do you want to do today? It's really nice outside."

"Ride my bike," Matt signed back.

But Haley and Carolyn looked at each other and just shrugged.

"We could start our club," suggested Carolyn, who only knows two signs — the ones for "flower" and "I'm sorry" — so Haley signed Carolyn's suggestion to Matt so that he would know what was going on.

When he heard about a girls' club, he made a face.

"How about going over to the Pikes'?" Jessi signed (speaking at the same time, of course, so that Carolyn wouldn't be left out of the conversation). "Mal's there sitting for Nicky, Vanessa, and Claire."

Haley and Carolyn looked at each other and grinned. Jessi knew they were thinking of talking to Vanessa about their club.

Matt grinned, too. He's become friends with the Pike boys and would be happy to see Nicky.

So Jessi called Mallory and they agreed that the kids could play together.

When Jessi and her charges arrived at the Pikes' they were greeted at the door by an exuberant Claire. "Let's play Sardines! Let's play Sardines!" she cried, jumping up and down.

Haley didn't know the sign for "sardine," so she finger spelled it to Matt. Then Claire and Vanessa had to explain what Sardines is, and a lot more signing went on. In the end, the girls seemed to have forgotten about the club. Sardines sounded much more interesting.

Have you ever played that game? If not, this is how it goes: It's a version of Hide-and-Seek, only you have *one* hider and all the other players are seekers. When a seeker finds the hider, he doesn't just win that round of the game, he hides *with* him. The next person to find the hiders hides with them, too, and so on until one seeker is left. That seeker is the loser and starts out the next round of the game as the hider. The tricky thing when you're the hider is finding a big enough hiding place in which to fit a whole lot of other people.

Jessi and Mal took the kids into the backyard. You can play Sardines indoors, but ever since the triplets broke a chair playing the game one rainy day, Mrs. Pike has said the game must be played outdoors. The kids didn't mind. It's easier to find big hiding places in the yard.

"Okay," said Haley, signing at the same time. "We'll say 'eeny-meeny-miny-moe' to see who'll hide first."

"Meeny-miny-mony-moo?" repeated Claire, and everyone giggled.

"No," said Haley. "Eeny-meeny-miny-moe. Here. Everyone stand in a circle and put one hand out. Mal or Jessi, will one of you come help us?"

Jessi stood in the middle of the circle.

"You know what to do?" asked Haley.

"Sure," said Jessi, and she recited, "Eeny-meeny-miny-moe. Catch a tiger by the toe. If he hollers let him go. Eeny-meeny-miny-*moe!*" As she recited, she went around the circle of kids, touching each of their hands in turn. When she got to that final *moe*, she was touching Vanessa, so Vanessa became the first hider.

"Okay," began Vanessa. "You guys all have

to stand on the patio facing the house and close your eyes. *Jessi* will count to a hundred. Then you can start looking for me."

This was a good arrangement since Claire can't count to a hundred yet, and it would eliminate any "speed-counting."

So Matt, Haley, Carolyn, Nicky, and Claire stood on the patio with their eyes closed while Jessi counted. Vanessa knew exactly where she wanted to hide, and it was a good choice, too — under the low branches of a pine tree. She made a dash for the tree, huddled herself against the trunk, and was well hidden before Jessi had even reached twenty. When Jessi finally called out, "One hundred!" she added, "Okay, open your eyes, you guys," and tapped Matt on the shoulder so he'd know the searching had begun.

Jessi got the feeling right away that the pine tree was a favorite hiding spot of Vanessa's, because Nicky and Claire made a beeline for it. But they managed to creep in without the others seeing them.

Haley, Matt, and Carolyn searched the yard high and low.

Not a sound came from the pine tree.

Matt looked under an overturned wheelbarrow.

Haley climbed up and looked in the Pikes' tree fort.

Carolyn peered behind the toolshed.

"Where *are* they?" Haley finally exclaimed — and Jessi and Mal heard a giggle from under the pine tree. It was Claire. She just couldn't help herself. Unfortunately, Haley heard the giggle and made a dash for the pine tree. Matt saw her and followed.

So Carolyn was left alone. That meant she was the next hider, and she chose the tree fort. Once again Claire's giggles gave the spot away when she found Carolyn.

"I think Claire should have to be the next hider, just for giggling," announced Nicky, when the kids had gathered in the yard again.

"I should not!" exclaimed Claire.

"Should too."

"Should not."

"Should too — monkey-breath."

For a moment, Claire looked as if she were going to cry. But then her giggles erupted again. Nicky laughed, too, and so did the others, even Matt, once Haley had finger spelled "monkey-breath" to him.

Matt was the next hider and he found a wonderful spot beneath the overturned wheelbarrow. Nobody could see a speck of him.

Also, nobody else could hide in there with him. Matt realized this too late when Claire discovered him. She made a huge racket and everyone saw her and came running.

No one would confess to being the last to have seen her.

"It wasn't me! It wasn't me!" everyone kept saying.

Then Nicky said that he was thirsty, so Mallory brought a pitcher of ice water and a stack of paper cups out to the back patio. Sardines was over. Claire drank her water and wandered over to the swing set. Nicky and Matt decided to hold batting practice. (They're members of Kristy's Krushers.) And Carolyn, Haley, and Vanessa sat on the patio with Jessi and Mal.

"Where's Marilyn?" Mal asked Carolyn.

Carolyn shrugged. "At home, I guess. She never plays with me anymore."

"I guess you've got your friends now and Marilyn's got hers," said Jessi.

Carolyn made a face. "Marilyn doesn't have any friends. She's too bossy."

"What about Gozzie Kunka?" asked Mal, who'd heard about her from Dawn and me.

"Who?!" exclaimed Haley.

"Gozzie Kunka. The foreign girl. The one who's new at your school."

"I never heard of anyone named Gozzie Kunka," said Haley, frowning.

"Me neither," said Vanessa.

"I have," said Carolyn. "I wouldn't exactly call her Marilyn's friend, but Marilyn's been talking about her a lot. She says she's been all around the world. Gozzie's father is with the government, only now they've settled down."

"You'd think a fancy family like that would settle down in Washington, D.C., or New York or some other big city," said Jessi. "Not in Stoneybrook, Connecticut."

The girls looked at each other and shrugged. Then Carolyn, Vanessa, and Haley decided to talk about their club. Half an hour later, Jessi took Matt, Haley, and Carolyn back to the Braddocks'. The kids waved good-bye to each other, a sign everyone understands.

As they left the Pikes' yard, Carolyn looked at Jessi and said, "Boy, will Daddy be proud of me when he finds out I'm learning sign language. Marilyn doesn't know a single sign, but I'm going to learn lots from Haley and Matt. I bet Marilyn will be jealous. . . . Really jealous."

CHAPTER 7

"*R*ain, rain, go away, and never come back another day*," sang Marilyn Arnold.

"That's *not* how the song goes," Carolyn informed her. "It's, *Rain, rain, go away. Come again some other day.*"

"I *know*. Sheesh. I was just thinking how nice it would be if the sun shone all the time. And the flowers were always blooming and — "

"That couldn't happen," said Carolyn, the science expert. "Flowers *can't* bloom all the time, especially if it never rains. And if it never rained, we'd run out of water. We wouldn't have any to drink or to take baths in, and everything would dry up and we'd all be dead."

"Would not."

"Would too."

"Would not."

"WOULD TOO!"

"WOULD NOT!!"

"Girls, *enough!*" I finally cried. I was baby-sitting at the Arnolds' house, and it was indeed a rainy day. I hadn't interrupted the girls' argument until now, because I'd been hoping they would work things out for themselves. But apparently they weren't going to.

"Well, Marilyn's being a pest," complained Carolyn, who was sitting on the floor of the Arnolds' rec room, taking things out of my Kid-Kit, one by one.

"I am *not.*" Marilyn turned away from the window where she'd been gazing out at the rain that had been falling steadily all day. "I just want to go outside. We were stuck indoors all day at school, even during recess."

"Yeah, but we got to play Seven-Up in our classrooms," said Carolyn.

"That's a dumb game."

"You're a dumb *person.*"

"You *guys!*" I cried. "What has gotten into you?"

"Nothing," they both said sullenly.

"Well, come on over here. Take a look in the Kid-Kit. There was a sale at Bellair's, and all us baby-sitters went to it and got some great new stuff. Here's a kaleidoscope. See? You can make neat patterns by looking through it." I held the kaleidoscope up to one eye and said, "Right now, I see a thousand Carolyns moving around."

"Great," muttered Marilyn.

"And I got some modeling clay," I went on. "Oh, and well, this didn't come from the store, but it's a board game. It's called 'Mary Anne's Game of School.' You roll the dice and have to do things like take extra gym or go to the principal's office or — here, if you land on this square, you get straight A's and you can move ahead ten whole spaces. The object of the game is to make it from September all the way around the board to June. The first person to do that is the winner." I was very proud of my game, in case you couldn't tell. It was the first game I'd invented, and I thought that any kid who was old enough to go to elementary school would like it. I had even found big buttons to use as playing pieces and I had carefully lettered a stack of cards that said things like, "Forgot gym suit. Move back one space." Or, "Teacher makes a mistake and you correct him. Move ahead two spaces."

Just as I'd hoped, the twins were intrigued by the game. They even seemed to forget about their argument and we set the game up on the floor. The twins sat across from each other, though; they wouldn't sit next to each other.

"Carolyn'll cheat if she can see my cards," said Marilyn.

"Marilyn'll cheat right back," said Carolyn.

(And I had thought they were through fighting.)

"Okay, how do we start?" asked Marilyn.

"We roll the dice to see who goes first," I replied.

The twins grabbed for the dice. Then they looked at me warily.

"Who gets to roll first?" asked Carolyn.

"Does it matter?" I replied.

"Yes, because I want to roll first," said Carolyn.

"So do I," said her sister.

I solved *that* problem. "*I'll* roll first," I said. "The person on my left — that's you, Carolyn — will go next."

"No fair!" cried Marilyn.

"Yes, it is. In most games, the players take their turns going clockwise. That's to the left."

Marilyn pouted and wasn't happy until she realized she'd rolled the highest number and would get to start the game. We played calmly for about ten minutes. Carolyn was winning, but Marilyn was taking it well. All was peaceful until Marilyn landed in the square Carolyn was in. When that happened she had to draw a card. It said, "Caught talking in class. The first person on the space moves back ten spaces."

"Ten spaces!" screeched Carolyn. "Marilyn, you — you have monkey-breath."

Marilyn's face turned an interesting shade of purple, but all she said was, "I'm through with this game. I'm going to my room."

"It's not *your* room, it's *our* room," Carolyn spat out, "and *I* want to go to it."

"Well, you can't, because I'm going. I said so first."

Carolyn paused. Then she murmured, "I hate sharing a room with you."

"I don't know why," replied Marilyn. "You're hardly ever there. You're hardly ever *home*. It might as well *be* my room."

"Well, it isn't."

You're probably wondering why I wasn't saying anything. It was because I was too surprised. I'd never heard the twins argue this badly before. They used to be nuisances to baby-sitters. They used to play tricks and confuse people, but they were always in on things together — even when they wanted desperately to be considered individuals. This was something new.

Then, before I could stop them, Marilyn and Carolyn (practically in the same breath) shouted, "*I'm* going to *my* room!"

They made a dash for the stairs, reached them at the same time, and struggled up them side by side, elbowing each other all the way.

At last I came to my senses. "Watch out, you two. Somebody's going to get hurt."

"I don't care!" the twins said together, as I dashed up the stairs after them. I was right on their heels, which was a good thing, because Carolyn reached their bedroom just a few steps ahead of Marilyn and tried to close the door in her face. Since I'm taller than the girls, I thrust my hands above Marilyn's head and held the door open.

Carolyn stomped to her bed and flopped onto it.

Marilyn stomped to *her* bed and flopped onto it.

Both of them faced the wall.

"Now listen, you guys," I said. "I need to know what's going on."

"Nothing," they replied for the second time that day.

"This is not 'nothing,' " I told them. "I want the truth."

There was a moment of silence. Then Marilyn said, "Carolyn's always going off and leaving me alone. She never plays with me anymore."

"*Marilyn* is always invading on me," Carolyn replied. "Or she used to. She never left me alone. And she bossed my friends around. So I stopped letting her come places with me."

(Both girls were still talking to the walls.)

"Besides," Marilyn went on, "Mommy likes Carolyn better because she has so many friends and she's so smart."

"And," said Carolyn, "Daddy likes Marilyn better because she can play the piano and she gets to be in recitals and last week she won an award."

I sighed. "You know what?" I said to the girls. "You are two different people now. You have different friends. You can't expect everyone to treat you the same anymore. Besides, your parents still love you both as much as ever."

Slowly Marilyn and Carolyn turned around. They looked at each other, but they didn't have the big emotional scene I'd been hoping for. I wanted them to hop off their beds, meet in the middle of their room, hug, cry, and apologize.

Instead, Marilyn said, "Well, if I'm so different from Carolyn, then I don't want her sharing *my* room."

Before Carolyn could even say, "It isn't *your* room, it's *ours*," which I knew she was going to do, Marilyn had marched to her desk, opened a drawer, and taken out a roll of masking tape. Then she stepped over to the window, which was in the middle of the room, placed the end of the tape on the exact center of the window, and ran the tape down the sill to the floor and across the rug to the opposite wall.

"There," she said. "This half is mine. That half is yours. *No crossing the line*, get it?"

I stood in the doorway and waited to see what would happen.

Carolyn smiled. "Got it. But how are you going to leave the room? The door's on my side of the tape. You're stuck in here."

Marilyn blushed, embarrassed. But then her face brightened. "I think you've got a bigger problem," she said. "The closet is on *my* side of the tape. You'll have to wear the clothes you've got on for the rest of your life."

I almost smiled. That would be a tragedy

for Carolyn, since she'd become so fashion conscious. It would kill her to wear the same clothes two days in a row, let alone the rest of her life.

"Okay, talk it out," I told the girls, leaning against the door jamb with my arms crossed. "You're old enough to figure out a compromise."

"No," said Marilyn.

"No," said Carolyn.

"No?" I repeated.

"I'm not talking to her," they said at the same time, each pointing to the other. Then they turned their backs and faced the walls again.

I was aghast. I'd always wanted a brother or a sister, especially a sister. And I'd thought it would be extra nice to have a twin sister. I had pictured ourselves sharing clothes, and talking late into the night (since we'd be *happily* sharing a room, of course). When we were younger we'd talk about imaginary things and what might be hiding under our beds. When we were older we'd talk about movies and our friends. When we were even older, we'd talk about boys and our parents.

Why, I wondered, couldn't Marilyn and Carolyn get along?

I stopped my wondering quickly, though. Mrs. Arnold would be home soon and I didn't want her to see the masking-tape divider down the center of the room. I asked Marilyn please to take it down.

She did — grumpily.

Once again I left two angry girls behind when I went home.

CHAPTER 8

I was so excited! It was the night of Dawn's mother's birthday dinner. Everything was planned, and Dad and Dawn and I sure hoped the surprise (actually surprises) would go off without any problems.

Mrs. Schafer's actual birthday was the next day, so she hadn't minded when this business associate of hers (who's also a friend of Dad's) had called and asked her out to dinner to discuss some work stuff. He said he would make a reservation in his name for two people at seven o'clock at Chez Maurice. Then he called and he *did* make a reservation, only it was for four people. Dad planned to drive Dawn and me to the restaurant (Dawn having told her mom that she was going to eat dinner with us again, which was *not* technically a lie), so that we would arrive by 6:45. Then Dad would say to the maitre d', "Hi, we're part of the Hum-

70

boldt party. We're a little early. But could we be seated now anyway?"

Then when Mrs. Schafer arrived, she'd say, "Hi, I'm with the Humboldt party," and the maitre d' would lead her to *our* table! Mr. Humboldt would never show up, of course.

That was how the evening would start — we hoped — and we had other things planned, too.

The surprise dinner was held on a Friday night, and Dawn and I were so excited all day that we couldn't think of anything except the dinner. At lunchtime, Dawn said, "Are you baby-sitting this afternoon, Mary Anne?"

"Nope," I replied. "Why?"

"Oh, good. I'm not, either. So I was thinking — after school we'll change into our going-out-to-dinner clothes. We'll wear them to the BSC meeting, and when the meeting is over, we can run right across the street to your house and be ready to go out for dinner. Your dad won't have to pick me up or anything."

Kristy rolled her eyes. I could hardly blame her. Dawn and I had been talking about the surprise dinner nonstop. But, well, it *was* awfully exciting.

And I had finally found a present for Mrs.

Schafer. I'd bought it with some of my baby-sitting money. It was jewelry, but it was *not* a cat. It was a charm that was a replica of the Stoneybrook High School ring. Kristy's brother Charlie had gotten it for me at the SHS store, where they sell school supplies and T-shirts and things like that. I thought Mrs. Schafer could wear it on a chain around her neck. I'd chosen it because I knew that years ago, when she and my father went to SHS, Dad hadn't been able to afford a school ring for either of them, so Mrs. Schafer had never gotten one. I figured the present would be full of meaning.

On Friday, for one of the very few times ever, Dawn and I could not *wait* for the BSC meeting to end. When it finally did, we felt just as if we'd slogged through another day at school. Claudia's digital clock flipped to six — and we were out of there!

" 'Bye, you guys!" we called over our shoulders as we tore down the Kishis' hallway and out the front door. Then we dashed across the street to my house.

Dad was already there. He'd come home early, and he greeted us at the door.

"Don't you two look nice," he said.

We grinned. "Thanks," I replied.

Dawn was wearing a flowered dress from the Laura Ashley store out at Washington Mall, and flat blue shoes. It was a rather un-Dawn outfit, but she looked very grown-up — and beautiful with all that long hair. I was wearing a green skirt and a baggy sweater with big, colorful flowers splashed over it, and beads in the centers of the flowers. Both of us had sat stiffly through the club meeting so as not to crush or wrinkle anything.

There was half an hour to kill before it was time to leave, but the three of us used the time well. Dawn and I brushed our hair and placed our presents in a small shopping bag. (I hadn't told Dawn what I'd bought for her mother.) Then we put on nail polish that Dawn had brought with her. I had to ask permission from Dad first, and he said I could wear clear only. Well, that was better than nothing, even if Dawn did get to wear purple.

Meanwhile, Dad called the restaurant, and a store that delivers balloon bouquets, to confirm several things. He put a single red rose in a wet napkin and put the napkin in a plastic bag. Then he added the rose to our shopping bag.

"Where's your gift?" I asked him.

"It's a secret," he replied mysteriously. "Come on. It's six-thirty. Time to go."

We reached Chez Maurice at 6:45 on the nose. So far so good. Then Dad told the maitre d' we were part of the Humboldt party, and we were led to a table right away.

It was beautiful! Just as we'd discussed, a bottle of champagne was chilling in a bucket by the table. Candles were lit, and on a pristine white tablecloth were fragile blue china plates and real silverware. While Dawn and I gawked at everything, Dad had a conference with the maitre d'. Then the maitre d' left and the three of us sat down. Dawn and I put our presents at Mrs. Schafer's place, and Dad unwrapped the rose and put it right *on* her plate. Everything looked so elegant.

"The only thing missing is the balloon bouquet," said Dad.

"And my mother," added Dawn.

We laughed.

Luckily the balloons arrived five minutes before Mrs. Schafer did. A waiter tied them to a chandelier over our table. I hoped the chandelier wouldn't get too hot because popping helium balloons at Chez Maurice would be pretty embarrassing.

The balloons had just been tied up and the

waiter had left when Mrs. Schafer was escorted to our table. When she saw the three of us, the balloons, the presents, the rose, and the champagne, I thought she was going to faint.

"Surprise! Happy birthday!" we said, but not very loudly.

"Oh, my goodness!" exclaimed Dawn's mom. She took her seat at the table a little shakily. "What happened to Stu Humboldt?"

Dad smiled. "Forget about him. There's no business dinner. Dawn and Mary Anne and I have had this planned for weeks," he said. Then he pinned the rose to Mrs. Schafer's blouse — and the two of them smiled at each other like they were the only two people in the restaurant.

A little while later, the waiter brought the menus, and the meal began. I won't go into too many details about the meal because, although it was fun and the food was great, the best part was yet to come.

Dessert.

As Dad had arranged with the maitre d', our waiter announced that he would bring us dessert menus, but instead he brought — a cake! No one sang "Happy Birthday," though, and I could tell Mrs. Schafer was relieved.

The cake was beautiful. The frosting was white with pink and blue flowers everywhere, and on top were four candles. We all leaned over for a closer look, but after Mrs. Schafer had blown out the candles, she continued to peer at the cake.

"What is it?" asked Dawn.

Very slowly, her mother pulled out one candle and held up something that had been slipped over it onto the cake.

"Is this what I think it is?" she asked my father.

He nodded nervously.

Mrs. Schafer held the something up for Dawn and me to see.

It was a diamond ring.

"It's — it's an engagement ring," she told us. Then she turned to Dad. "I thought we agreed — no rings. We've both been through this marriage business before. We don't need new rings."

Dad shrugged. "I just couldn't help myself," he said, "especially since I couldn't even get you a school ring back in twelfth grade."

Mrs. Schafer leaned over and kissed my father on the cheek. And as you can imagine, Dawn and I just gaped at them. Finally I managed to whisper, "You mean you're getting married?"

My father and Dawn's mother nodded.

"We were trying to think of a special way to tell you, but we hadn't come up with anything," said Dad. "I decided this might be the best way — a celebration." He turned to Mrs. Schafer. "I'm sorry I didn't consult you. Do you mind?"

"Only a little," she replied honestly. "How can I mind too much with balloons and a cake and — and a ring . . ."

I could tell she was about to cry so I started to say, "Open your presents."

Instead, Dawn looked at me and said in amazement, "We're going to be *step*sisters! Can you believe it?"

Suddenly *I* began to cry. Dawn did, too. We threw our arms around each other. Then we asked our parents a million questions, such as when would the wedding be held, would we be in it, and could we invite our friends?

Dad and Mrs. Schafer didn't have too many answers, except that the wedding would probably be a small one, held very soon, and that Jeff would fly in from California for it.

After that, Mrs. Schafer opened her presents. She loved Dawn's day-planner, even though it was no surprise and, as you can imagine, she *really* loved the school-ring charm I'd gotten her. She almost started to cry again, but instead she said, "What a special gift, honey. I'm so glad you're going to be my stepdaughter."

Dad smiled at me.

I grinned at Dawn.

Dawn took her time smiling back.

After that, the party wasn't *quite* so festive. But it wasn't until I was snug in bed that night, Tigger curled up next to my head, that some other things began to bother me. For instance, Dawn had said her mother doesn't like cats. Well, no way was I giving up Tigger. Somehow, Mrs. Schafer would have to learn to get along with him after the wedding. Then I thought about what a neatnik my father is, and how organized he is. He likes everything just so. How would he ever live with Dawn's messy, scatterbrained mother?

Oh, well, those were small things, I told myself, compared to the fact that I was going to gain a stepmother, a part-time stepbrother, and . . . a stepsister. And the stepsister would be Dawn — one of my best friends in the whole world. I could not believe my good luck!

CHAPTER 9

Dawn and I learned our amazing news on a Friday night. Somehow, we managed to wait all the way until the Monday BSC meeting before we told any of our other friends about it. I honestly don't know how we did that. Sheer willpower, I guess. Also, we really wanted to make a splash. That was the best way we could think of to do that.

I even asked Kristy if Logan could come to the meeting.

"Why?" she asked.

Good question. "Because I have some news," I replied carefully, "and I want all my closest friends to hear it at once." (I purposely didn't say that *Dawn* and I had news. That might have given the secret away.)

"We-ell," said Kristy slowly, "it's not our usual club policy, but sure — if Logan can come, he's welcome."

"Thanks," I replied. I already knew that Logan could come. I'd told him to hold five-thirty till six open on Monday in case we asked him to attend the meeting.

At five-thirty on Monday afternoon, Dawn and I were just as beside ourselves as we'd been at Friday's meeting.

"What is it with you two?" asked Kristy testily. "You've *got* to keep your minds on the meeting. This club is a formal organization, you know."

"We know, we know," said Dawn breathlessly. "We also know there'll be lulls after we've finished our business and in between calls. And Mary Anne and I have something very important to tell you."

"So you're part of this, too?" Kristy asked Dawn, and I could see the hurt in her eyes. I was Kristy's best friend, but lately Dawn and I had been having all the excitement and secrets.

"Well, yes," said Dawn, as if she were making some great confession.

Kristy sighed. "All right. Let's get this meeting underway. Order, order!"

I looked around Claud's room. We were all in place — Kristy in the director's chair; Stacey backwards in the desk chair; Claudia, Dawn, and I lined up on Claud's bed; and Jessi and Mal on the floor. The few times Logan had attended meetings, he'd sat wherever he could find a space, usually next to me. But on that afternoon, he was also sitting on the floor, leaning against Claud's closet door.

Since it was a Monday, Stacey collected club dues. (Logan doesn't have to pay.) When she was finished, we just sat in our places. The phone did not ring. Dawn and I looked at each other. Now was our chance.

Dawn opened her mouth, and —

Ring, ring!

"I'll get it!" screeched Kristy, reaching for the phone.

It was Mrs. Perkins, across the street. Kristy and I arranged for Mallory to sit for the girls a week from Wednesday.

When the phone was quiet, Dawn and I looked at each other again.

Dawn opened her mouth.

Ring, ring!

This time Stacey answered the phone and set up a job with the Rodowsky boys.

The phone grew quiet.

Dawn and I looked at each other.

We did not say a word.

"What are you waiting for?" asked Kristy.

"The phone," replied Dawn. "If I start to say something, it'll ring again."

But it didn't ring for a full minute, so at last Dawn said, "Mary Anne? Should I give it a try?"

I nodded.

Then Dawn looked across the room at Logan. She looked back at me. "You tell the news," she said unexpectedly.

I knew why she had decided to let me tell. She felt that Logan ought to hear such important news from me. Also, I'd known most of the other BSC members a lot longer than she had. I smiled gratefully at my future stepsister.

"Okay, here goes," I said, fully expecting the phone to ring again, but it didn't. "On Friday night, when we took Dawn's mom out for her birthday, it turned out that there was a surprise for Dawn and me, too. A *big* one."

"There *was*?" said Claudia.

I nodded. "Dad's present to Mrs. Schafer was an engagement ring. They're going to get married. Dawn and I will be stepsisters!"

Well, you have never heard such loud silence. Everyone in the room was stunned, but only for a moment. Then this incredible shrieking and cheering and yelling began. Logan jumped up, crossed the room in two strides (nearly stepping on Mallory), grabbed me off the bed, and whirled me around. As soon as he put me down, Claudia gave me a huge hug. Dawn and Stacey hugged. Everyone hugged — except Kristy. I mean, she *did* get into the spirit of things, but it took her a little while longer. I knew that deep down, she was hurt, and I'd been expecting that. How could she not feel hurt? Something had just happened over which she had absolutely no control and which was going to form a unique bond between Dawn and me forever. So I was prepared for Kristy's reaction. When she finally did hug me, I managed to slip a note into the back pocket of her jeans. It read:

Dear Kristy,
As you and I grow up, we'll have lots of friends — and lots of things will change. But one thing can never change: you were my very first best friend.
I love you. Mary Anne.

I hoped Kristy would find the note before she threw her jeans in the wash. (As it happened, she did. She never said anything to

83

me, but I could tell she'd read the note by the way she smiled at me in school the next day. I felt really good about that.)

Anyway, the eight of us were making such a racket that Claudia's genius sister, Janine, actually dragged herself away from her computer and came down the hall to see what was going on.

"Is anything wrong?" she yelled from the doorway. "What's happening? You're making quite a bit of noise. Furthermore, your phone is ringing."

"What?" shouted Kristy. "The phone?"

Janine nodded.

"Hey! Everyone be quiet!" ordered Kristy, as Janine disappeared back into her room, which is like the Bermuda Triangle, since she hardly ever comes out of it.

We quieted down enough to set up another job. Then the questions began flying:

"When will the wedding be?"

"Was your mom surprised, Dawn?"

"Does Jeff know yet?"

And the exclamations, too:

"I can't believe you won't be an only child anymore, Mary Anne!"

"You're finally going to have a mother!"

"You guys are going to be *step*sisters. Awesome!"

Dawn and I, bit by bit, told everyone the story of the birthday dinner. We answered their questions as well as we could, even though we didn't know much more than they did. Some of those nagging thoughts (like Mrs. Schafer not liking cats) came back to me as we talked things over, but I put them out of my mind.

The next job call was from Mrs. Arnold, which prompted Jessi to ask me how the twins were doing.

"You know, I think they're worse," I had to admit. I reminded my friends about the masking-tape incident, which they'd read about in the club notebook. "The girls are *so* different now it's unbelievable. They vie for their parents' attention, they're mean to each other, and this business of Carolyn having all these friends has really come between them."

"In fami — " said Mal, at the same time Kristy said, "The twins — "

We laughed. Then, "You go first," Kristy told Mallory.

"Well, I was just going to say," Mal began,

"that in families, brothers and sisters don't *always* get along."

"That's true," said Jessi. "Becca and I fight sometimes. Sometimes we even get mad at Squirt."

"Yeah," agreed the rest of us, except for Stacey and me, since we had never had a brother or sister not to get along with.

"And kids in families always tease," Mal went on, "no matter how much they love each other. Sometimes the target of the worst teasing can change. In my family, it used to be Vanessa. I guess because she would make such a pest out of herself by always talking in rhyme. Now a lot of the teasing is directed at Nicky. And when I first got my braces, the triplets called me 'metal-mouth' for two weeks. Just wait until *they* get *their* braces."

"But what about this business with their parents?" I asked. "That's new. And I don't like it."

"Well, what I was going to say," said Kristy, "is that the twins are changing. We know that. And their mother and father are two different people, of course, so now I bet the girls are trying to do things that will please one or the other of their parents. Like, maybe Mrs. Arnold really appreciates kids who are social and have lots of friends. And maybe Mr. Arnold really appreciates artsy stuff like music or whatever."

"That makes sense," I said.

"It can work in reverse, too," Kristy pointed out. "Sometimes parents bend over backwards trying to please their *kids.* I'll never forget when Mom and Watson first got married. Any time there was an argument or a problem, Mom sided with Karen and Andrew, and Watson sided with my brothers and me. They just wanted their stepkids to like them."

I nodded.

"Plus," went on Kristy, "you know how friends can go off in different directions?"

"Yeah," I said guiltily.

"Well, if friends can, then I guess twin sisters can, too. But I bet things will work out again after awhile."

"I think they usually do," added Mal. "Between brothers and sisters, or parents and kids, or friends."

The eight of us grew so quiet thinking these things over that I could hear Janine's computer clicking away in her room.

Then Claudia suddenly exclaimed, "Oh, my lord! I just can't believe you two are going to be stepsisters!"

"*And* friends *and* club members," I pointed out.

That was all it took for the screaming and hugging to start again.

Logan couldn't take it any longer. "See y'all tomorrow," he said hastily, and escaped.

It didn't matter. It was almost six o'clock anyway.

As you can imagine, the rest of the "meeting" was just giggling and talking. Kristy didn't even seem to mind — much.

CHAPTER 10

Saturday

I am up to my ears with the subject of sibling rivalry. First the Arnold twins, now my own brothers and sisters -- the younger ones, I mean. I baby-sat for Karen, Andrew, David Michael, and Emily today while Nannie went to bowling practice, Mom and Watson went to visit friends in Titusville (friends who didn't want a bunch of kids along, I guess), Charlie headed for a used-car lot to buy his first car (Mom had given him permission), and Sam went with him to help him pick it out. (A friend of theirs, Patrick, went along to drive Mom's car home afterward.)

I can't say that the afternoon got off to a good start, because it didn't. Karen was already in a rotten mood, and things went downhill from there.

Why was Karen in a rotten mood? According to Kristy, it was because Emily had had the audacity that morning to tug at Kristy's arm, hand her Andrew's battered copy of *The Teddy Bears' Picnic*, and say, "Read?"

And then Kristy had had the audacity to reply, "Sure, Emily," and lead her into the den, sit down, pull her onto her lap, and read the story to her.

That was all it took. Apparently, Karen was already in a bad mood, but reading together *is* a special activity for Karen and Kristy, so on that particular day, Karen wasn't thrilled to see Emily and her big sister sharing a teddy-bear moment.

Kristy's mom noticed and offered to read *The Witch Next Door* to Karen, which is her favorite book, but Karen would have none of it.

"No, thank you," she said haughtily. Then she stalked up to her room.

By the afternoon, Karen was in an even worse mood. She had spent the morning muttering about what pains and brats little sisters are.

"They are always in your way," she'd said as she tried to pass Emily on the stairs. Emily was climbing them one slow step at a time, holding onto the banister with one hand, and trailing her blanket behind her with the other.

"They get all the attention," she said at lunchtime as Watson cut Emily's sandwich into quarters for her, and Nannie settled Emily in her high chair.

By the time Watson and Kristy's mom and everyone else were taking off, leaving Kristy in charge, Karen had marched up to her room, marched back down again holding her T-shirt that reads, "I'm the middle sister . . . and proud of it," and said, "See this? I don't want it anymore. You can put it in Shannon's dog-bed." Then she had dropped the shirt on the floor and huffed off to the den to be alone for awhile.

"I'm sorry to leave you with this mess," Watson apologized as he and Mrs. Brewer headed for his car.

"That's okay. I can handle it," Kristy assured him. She turned around and walked back into the house. She passed Andrew and David Michael, who were in the living room with the curtains closed, playing a game in the dark called The Wandering Frog People. The Pike boys made the game up.

Kristy was watching them and smiling when she heard an odd noise from the direction of the kitchen — several small thumps, like something being dropped. Then she heard Karen say, "Bad girl, Emily. Bad girl!"

Kristy raced to the kitchen. There was Karen, shaking her finger at Emily, who was standing by a chair. On the table was a package of cookies, and on the floor were several broken ones.

"Just look what Emily did," said Karen in a disgusted voice. "She made a huge mess. Daddy hates cookie crumbs on the floor. Plus, Emily tried to climb up to the table for the cookies when she *knows* she's not supposed to stand on chairs."

Kristy looked firmly at Emily. Watson, Kristy's mother, and Nannie had all said that it was important not to spoil Emily, even though she had gotten off to a bad start in life. And yet — Kristy didn't know what to think. Emily couldn't talk well enough to defend herself.

"Did you try to get the cookies?" Kristy asked Emily.

Emily just stood there and cried.

"Did you *break* the cookies?" This time Kristy pointed to the mess on the floor.

More tears from Emily, while Karen watched, hands on hips.

"If I did something bad, Kristy," said Karen, "Daddy or Elizabeth would send me to my room. They always do."

That was true. But Kristy still didn't know for sure what had happened. Finally she just said, "Emily, did you do something naughty?"

Emily's crying grew louder, so Kristy decided that meant she was guilty. "Okay," Kristy continued. "Up to your room."

She marched Emily to her room, took off her shoes, and put her in her crib. "Time-out for ten minutes," she told her. Then, feeling horrible as Emily stood in her crib, crying hopelessly, Kristy turned and walked away. By the time she'd returned to the kitchen, Karen had cleaned up the mess, but now *she* was crying.

"What's the matter?" asked Kristy, thoroughly perplexed. "You can't possibly be upset that I punished Emily."

"Yes I am," wailed Karen.

Kristy sat down. *"Why?"* she demanded. Nothing made sense.

"Because you should be punishing *me. I*

made the mess. Then I blamed it on Emily. I just wanted to see if you'd really punish her. I know what I did was wrong. Emily looked so sad and — and confused. She even looked a little mad. Do you think she understood what I did to her?"

"She might have," Kristy replied. "Emily's not stupid. She just doesn't talk much yet. And furthermore, Karen Brewer," (Kristy had stopped herself just in time from saying "young lady," a phrase her mother uses that she hates), "furthermore, you will now have ten minutes of time-out in your room while I try to explain things to Emily. Then I want you to apologize to her."

Karen nodded. She knew she deserved everything that was happening. So now Kristy walked Karen up the stairs. On their way, David Michael called out, "Kristy, I'm going over to Linny's house!"

"Okay," Kristy replied. She noted that the living room curtains had been pulled back and that Andrew was on the floor, playing with Shannon. The Wandering Frog People must have come to an end.

Kristy deposited Karen in her room, then rescued Emily from her crib, saying, "I'm sorry, I'm sorry." She held Emily in the rocking chair for awhile and tried to explain what had happened. By the time Karen's punishment was over, Emily was smiling again, so Kristy took her into Karen's room.

"Time's up," she informed Karen.

Karen nodded.

"Now don't you have something to say to your sister?"

"Yes," replied Karen. "I want to say — Hey, get out of my toy box, Emily!"

"*Karen,*" said Kristy warningly.

"Well, she's always getting into my stuff. And she's doing it right now."

"She just wants to see what's in the box. She isn't going to hurt anything."

"How do you know?"

Kristy didn't know. But luckily for everybody, just at that moment, Emily emerged from the box with an old stacking toy of Karen's.

"Where'd that come from?" asked Karen. "That's a baby toy. I didn't even know it was in there."

Emily sat on the floor and happily placed the colored rings on the pole. Karen got up and dug through her toy box. At the bottom she found a pull-toy, some plastic pop-apart beads, and a cloth book about a little girl who takes a bath.

Karen set them in front of Emily. "Here," she said. "You can have these. I don't need them anymore." Then she added, "I'm sorry I yelled at you, Emily."

Well, the grin that lit up Emily's face could have melted the heart of Ebenezer Scrooge (before he came to his senses, that is).

Kristy sighed, glad the crisis was over and that she could relax and enjoy baby-sitting.

That's what she thought. Little did she know that another crisis was about to arise. It all began when, sometime later, she, Andrew, Emily, and Karen heard, *Honk, honk!*

"I bet that's Charlie!" cried Andrew. "I bet he's got his new car."

"His old car," Karen corrected him.

"His new old car," said Kristy.

Kristy and the kids rushed out the front door. In the driveway before them was a clinker of a car. In fact, it looked a lot like Nannie's Pink Clinker, except that it wasn't pink. It was sort of gray. And Kristy could see a scratch and two dents just on the passenger's side of the car. Plus, the fenders were rusting.

But Charlie was obviously very proud of his

car. He and Sam climbed out of it just as Patrick, Charlie's friend, pulled up in Mrs. Brewer's station wagon.

Charlie grinned and waved to the crowd on the porch. "Well, here it is," he said. "One gorgeous piece of metal."

One gorgeous piece of junk, thought Kristy, imagining what her mother and Watson would say when they laid eyes on it.

"It may not actually be *gorgeous*," Charlie went on, "but it runs like a dream, and with a little paint and some wax I can really fix it up. You guys can help me."

"Oh, thank you so much," said Kristy sarcastically.

Charlie was too excited to notice. "Come on, everyone. We're going for a ride," he announced. "We have to drive Patrick home." And with that he took Emily's car seat out of the station wagon, attached it to the backseat of his car, and loaded Emily, Andrew, and Karen inside. Then Sam and Patrick piled in. "You coming, Kristy?" asked Charlie.

"I can't," she replied. "David Michael's over at Linny's. I'll have to wait for him here."

"Okay," Charlie said, and drove off.

Five minutes later, David Michael returned. When he found out where everyone was, he pitched a fit right in the front yard.

"You mean my own brother got a new car and he took everyone for a ride but *me?* His own brother?"

"David Michael — " Kristy began. She was going to explain that Patrick had needed a ride home, and everyone else had been standing right there by the car. But David Michael had already banged into the house. When he came out a few moments later, he was carrying a big piece of paper and a fat black Magic Marker. In huge letters he wrote on the paper:

NO PARKING

He posted the sign on a tree in front of the house where Charlie couldn't miss it.

Charlie didn't miss it. He took the hint, too. He let the other kids out of his car and then took David Michael on a special ride of his own.

Kristy hoped the sibling rivalry problems were over for awhile.

CHAPTER 11

One Saturday evening, Dad invited Dawn and her mom over for dinner. That wasn't unusual, except that this time he said, "We ought to discuss the wedding. We should set a date, if nothing else, and we want the two of you involved in everything."

Oh, goody! I thought. Immediately I wondered how long it would take Dawn and me to agree on matching bridesmaids' dresses. I knew I would probably want something fancier than Dawn would want. I pictured myself in a long pale pink dress with a lace collar. Maybe a straw hat would look nice, too. I'd seen a picture of a bridesmaid in an outfit just like that. A pink ribbon had been tied around the hat and it hung down the girl's back. Would Dawn go for something like that? Probably not. On the other hand, she *had* bought that Laura Ashley dress, so there was hope.

"Mary Anne?" Dad was saying.

"What? I mean, yes?" I wondered how many times he'd called my name.

"What about dinner? We don't need to do anything fancy. I think our choices tonight are fish or the rest of that vegetable casserole."

I made a face. "Could we order in Chinese food? The Schafers can always find vegetarian things on the menu."

"Well . . . all right," replied my father.

"Oh, great! Thank you!" I kissed Dad.

"Do you want to call Dawn and just check to make sure Chinese food is all right with her and her mother?"

"Okay," I answered. So I did and it was.

The Schafers came over around six-thirty. We were all hungry, so Dad found the menu right away, but then we couldn't decide what to order. We tossed around suggestion after suggestion. At *last* we decided on cold sesame noodles (yum), eggplant in garlic sauce (yuck — let the Schafers eat that), sweet and sour pork (that was for Dad and me), and something called Imperial Vegetables Oriental that even I said I'd eat.

While we waited for the food to arrive, Dad and Mrs. Schafer sat on the couch in the living room and talked. I noticed that these days, even when Dawn and I were around, they sat much closer together than they used to. Dawn and I sat on the floor and talked, too. I told her about my idea for the bridesmaids' dresses. I even showed her the picture, which I found tucked away in one of my desk drawers.

Dawn looked thoughtful. Then she smiled. I thought she was going to laugh at the dresses.

"I do not find them *that* funny," I said testily.

But Dawn said, "It isn't that. They're not funny. It's just that we haven't been asked to be bridesmaids yet."

"Oh, yeah," I replied. Then we both started laughing.

At that point, the food arrived.

"Thank heavens," said Mrs. Schafer. "I'm starving."

My dad and Dawn's mom each paid the delivery guy for half of our order. Then we took the bags into the kitchen, opened the cartons of food, filled our plates, sat down at the table, and began eating. When we were slightly less hungry Dad said, "Okay. About the wedding."

"Which church is it going to be in?" asked Dawn immediately.

"Yeah," I said. "I know we don't go to church very often, Dad, but ours is so pretty. And it's got the longest aisle of any church in Stoneybrook."

"That's important," said Dawn, "because, Mom, your train will look gorgeous going up and down a long aisle."

"And we can have flowers by the altar," I added.

"White orchids," said Dawn.

"Pink azalea branches — to go with our *bridesmaids' dresses*," I said pointedly.

My father and Mrs. Schafer had stopped eating and were just staring at each other. They didn't say a word.

"And, Dad," I went on, "the ushers should wear gray striped bowties. I saw that in a movie once and they looked *so handsome*."

"And, Mom," said Dawn, "you and Mary Anne and I should go to Rita's Bridal Shoppe out at Washington Mall. They make wedding gowns and bridesmaids' dresses to order. I know that for a fact. Oh, and get a beaded veil."

"And, Dad, could you please *rent* a tux?" I asked him. "Don't wear your old one. The pants are too short. And don't refer to it as a monkey suit in front of any of my friends, okay?"

"Gosh, Jeff will need a tux, too," said Dawn. "Maybe his should match the ushers'. Or do the ushers just wear suits? And what will Jeff be in the wedding? The ring bearer?"

My father and Dawn's mother were still neither eating nor talking. Before one of them could answer Dawn, I exclaimed, "Oh, please, can we have a little bride and groom on top of the wedding cake? Tasteful ones, I mean."

"And we better have a four-tier cake," added Dawn. "That way, you can save the top tier for yourselves, like they do in books, and there'll still be enough cake for all the guests. By the way, where are we going to hold the reception?"

"Could we have it in that big room at Chez Maurice?" I asked. "That would be so meaningful. I wonder how many people can fit in there. Fifty? A hundred?"

"Depends if we're going to have a sit-down dinner or just a big party," Dawn answered.

"Oh, hey! I mean, oh," I said. "I just thought of something else. Who'll be the flower girl? We don't have any little sisters or girl cousins."

"Myriah Perkins?" suggested Dawn. "Or Gabbie? Or Claire or Margo Pike?"

"Whoever it is," I said, "her dress should be similar to ours, like Karen's was similar to Kristy's when Kristy's mom and Watson got married."

Our parents finally found their voices. "Now wait a — " Dad began, just as Mrs. Schafer said, "Girls — "

They glanced at each other, holding a quick conversation with their eyes. At last Dawn's mom said, "Girls, we aren't going to have a wedding or a reception."

"What?" I cried.

"You *aren't?"* exclaimed Dawn. "Why not?"

"We just don't want one," said Dad. "We've each had one before, and this time around we don't think it's necessary."

"But Kristy's mother — " I started to say.

"Kristy's mother and Watson Brewer are different people," replied my father. "Besides, not even they had a wedding like the one you're talking about. Do you know how expensive a big wedding and reception would be these days?"

"Girls, we've talked this over," said Mrs. Schafer, "and we've decided we'd rather save the money for your college educations."

"Darn," said Dawn sulkily. "I was hoping to get to ride through Stoneybrook in a limo."

Everyone stopped talking for a moment. We'd stopped eating, too. After awhile, I said plaintively, "No wedding at *all?*"

"Not exactly *no* wedding," Dad told me. "We want to be married by the justice of the peace in a civil service in the courthouse. We want you girls and Jeff there, of course, and then we thought the five of us could go out for a quiet dinner."

"How about a compromise?" suggested Dawn pleadingly. "Couldn't you have a teeny wedding in the chapel of a church?"

"Then we could invite just a *few* people," I said. "Our friends will want to come. And Mrs. Schafer, don't you think that at least your parents would want to be there?"

"You wouldn't have to wear a wedding gown," Dawn told her mother.

"And you could just wear a nice suit," I said to Dad.

"And Mary Anne and I wouldn't even need to get new dresses," added Dawn.

(I elbowed her. I was always looking for an excuse to get a new dress.)

"Well," said Mrs. Schafer thoughtfully, "I suppose a *small* wedding — *very* small," she emphasized, "might be okay." She raised her eyebrows at Dad.

"I suppose," he said.

"We'd keep the guest list *really* small," I promised. "Just our closest friends — that's Kristy, Claud, Stacey, Jessi, Mal, and Logan."

"And then," said Dawn, "there would be Jeff, our grandparents, and maybe each of you would want to ask a couple of people from work. All together, including the four of us, that would probably be less than twenty people."

"If it's that small," said Dad, "maybe we could all go out to dinner afterwards. But no cake and no wedding gifts. Nothing but a dinner."

"That's do-able," said Dawn, and we all laughed.

"We're sorry to disappoint you girls," Mrs. Schafer said a moment later. "We had no idea you wanted a fancy wedding. It's a nice idea, but it's not what *we* want."

"Are you at least going on a honeymoon?" asked Dawn.

"Sort of," Dad answered. "Your mother and I will spend the night after the wedding at the Strathmoore Inn. Then maybe we could take a family vacation in the summer. We'll ask Jeff to join us, of course."

"You want *us* along on your honeymoon?" I squeaked.

"Mary Anne, that won't *be* the actual honeymoon. As I said before — "

"I know. You've already been through this."

"Right."

We finished our dinner then, managing to decide on a date for the wedding. Later, when the kitchen had been cleaned up, Dawn and I went to my room to talk things over.

"I can't believe we won't get to be in the wedding after all," I said, flopping down on the bed and staring at the ceiling.

"Yeah, what a drag," agreed Dawn. "Oh, well. At least we won't have to wear those awful pink dresses you saw."

I yanked the pillow out from under my head and threw it at Dawn. She wasn't expecting that, and it hit her in the face. We started giggling. Dawn threw the pillow back at me. More giggling.

"I am so glad we're going to be stepsisters," I said.

"Me, too. In fact, I think we'll be more like regular sisters. We'll be the closest sisters ever.

I think we should share my bedroom instead of having separate ones."

What? What had Dawn said?

I sat up. "What did you just say?" I demanded.

"I said I think we should *share* my bedroom."

"*Your* bedroom?"

"Yeah. When you and your dad move into our house."

I just stared at Dawn. I stared at her until her face fell.

"Uh-oh," she said. "Hasn't your father told you yet?"

"No," I replied coldly. "He hasn't."

CHAPTER 12

"Uh-oh," said Dawn again.

"Is that all you can say? 'Uh-oh'?" I was incensed. Dawn was still sitting on the floor, so I slid off the bed and stood up, towering over her. "Who made that decision?" I cried. "Who made it? And how come you know about it already and no one told me? How come I wasn't asked where I want to live? I suppose we'll have to get rid of Tigger, won't we, since your mother hates cats so much. And how come *I* have to leave *my* house? I grew up here. You just moved to Stoneybrook. You've only lived in your house for a little over a year."

"Whoa," said Dawn. "I'm sorry. Really I am. I thought your dad had told you about the move, because — "

"Well, he hadn't. And furthermore, how are we supposed to fit all our furniture into your house? It's already full of your furniture. I guess my dad and I have to give ours away, but you get to keep yours, right?"

Dawn's eyes had filled with tears. "I don't know," she said in a wavery voice. She brushed at one of her eyes with the back of her hand.

"This is the most unfair thing I have ever heard of!" I exploded.

I must have been talking awfully loudly. For one thing, Tigger had long since fled from the room. For another, Dad and Mrs. Schafer had appeared in the doorway.

"Girls," said Dad, and I could tell he was trying hard to control his voice, "what on earth is the matter?"

"I'll tell you what's the matter," I replied in a tone that surprised even myself. I *never* blow up at Dad or talk to him sharply. "*She*," (I pointed to Dawn), "has just informed me that you and I are moving out of our house and into *hers*. Apparently everyone knew except me. How come Dawn knew? Huh? How come she knew already? Well, I'll tell you one thing — no, I'll tell you two things. One, I am not getting rid of Tigger no matter how much *she*," (this time I pointed to Mrs. Schafer), "hates cats. And two, I don't have to like this decision or be nice about it. So there." I crossed my arms and sat down on my bed so hard I was afraid I'd break it. Oh, well. What would that have mattered? I'd be getting one of the Schafers' beds soon enough.

Needless to say, everyone looked stunned, even Tigger, who was peeping cautiously into my room. At last Mrs. Schafer said, "Come on, Dawn. I think it's time for us to go."

Dawn was crying hard by then, but I didn't care. Let her. At least she got to keep her house.

Mrs. Schafer put her arm around Dawn as they were leaving. "Mary Anne," she said softly, "I'm sorry you found out this way. We didn't mean for this to happen. And please let me assure you that Tigger will be welcome in our house." Then she led Dawn out of the room, saying over her shoulder to my father, "Call me later tonight, okay?"

"All right," replied Dad quietly. Then he sat next to me on the bed.

I was still so mad that I burst out, "You better have a good explanation for this," which is something he has said to me a number of times.

Dad didn't even get angry at me for being so rude. He just started talking. "Mary Anne,

I knew you'd be upset about the arrangement," he began. "That's why I hadn't told you yet. I was trying to figure out the right way and time to do it. But it *is* the best arrangement. You see, it makes much more sense for us to move into the Schafers' house than for them to move into ours. Theirs is bigger. Dawn and Jeff can keep their rooms, and you'll have a room of your own, too. That guest bedroom upstairs will become yours, and the den downstairs can be used when we have guests. You can move all of your furniture into the guest bedroom. You can decorate it so that it looks just like your old room, or you can redecorate it any way you want.

"But if the Schafers moved in here," Dad went on, "you and Dawn would have to share a room when Jeff came to visit. Also, we have fewer rooms than the Schafers do, and they have a bigger yard, as well as the barn for Jeff to play in. It just makes sense for the smaller family with the smaller house to move in with the bigger family with the bigger house. You can see that, can't you?"

"What about Tigger?" was my only reply.

"You heard what Dawn's mother said. Tigger will be welcome."

"But Mrs. Schafer doesn't like cats."

"That's true. But no matter where we lived she'd have to put up with him. He's part of the package. He comes with our family."

"Okay."

Tigger stepped carefully into my room then, stepped delicately over to the bed, and jumped into my lap.

"How come Dawn knew we were moving before I did?" I asked. I felt a little calmer.

"That was my fault," Dad replied. "When Sharon and I made the decision that we would move into her house, we each agreed to tell our children separately. She must have told Dawn, and probably Jeff, right away. But I knew the news would be difficult for you so I put off telling you. Finally, I put it off for too long, I guess. But Dawn didn't know that."

I could feel tears slipping down my cheeks. "I don't want to move," I whispered. "I grew up here. Claudia's always been across the street from me. Kristy used to live next door. I could look out my window and right into hers. When Kristy moved away and the Perkinses moved in, I showed Myriah how we could look in each other's windows. She'll miss that. And I'll be further away from Logan, further away from school, further away from everything — except Dawn's haunted secret passage."

Dad smiled. "Mary Anne, that passage is not haunted. It's not even secret anymore, since we all know about it."

I tried to smile, too. Then Dad folded me into his arms and gave me a big hug. I felt safe — but I still didn't want to move.

By the next day, I was relieved that Dad had been so nice about my outburst, but I was still angry. I barely spoke to Dawn in school. Lunchtime was especially tough. We had to pretend to act happy whenever one of our friends brought up the wedding or the business of becoming stepsisters. But neither of us said anything about my moving to Dawn's house.

And when Dawn whispered to me, "You know, my mother doesn't *hate* cats. She just doesn't like them much," I replied, "She does too hate them."

That was the end of that conversation.

As you can imagine, I was not in a great mood when I arrived at the Arnolds' house for a sitting job that afternoon. I would never in a million years have taken my feelings out on the girls, but I was hoping that maybe they would be an amusing change of pace.

No such luck. At least, not at first. Mrs. Arnold told me as she was putting on her coat that Marilyn was in the living room, practicing for a piano recital, and that Carolyn was up in the girls' bedroom. Something in her voice implied . . . trouble.

After Mrs. Arnold left, I decided not to interrupt Marilyn (who was playing quite loudly and with a lot of force), and to see what Carolyn was up to instead.

The first thing I saw in the twins' bedroom was that the masking-tape divider was back. I guessed that was why Marilyn was downstairs practicing so loudly. She was angry because she couldn't enter her own room. She'd have had to cross Carolyn's side first.

"Hi," I said to Carolyn. "Your mom just left."

"Okay." Carolyn went back to *Baby Island*, the book she was reading.

"I guess you're mad at your sister again, aren't you?"

"You mean Jerk-Face?"

"No, I mean Marilyn."

"Same thing."

"Look," I said. "You two cannot go on fighting forever. What's the problem this time?"

"I said I was inviting Haley over to play, so then Marilyn said she was inviting Gozzie over to play."

"So?"

"We wanted to play separately."

"Couldn't you and Haley — or Marilyn and Gozzie — have played outdoors while the others played indoors?"

"No. We both wanted to play in our *room*."

I sat thoughtfully on Marilyn's bed. "You know what's wrong here?" I said. "You and Marilyn are *very* different people now. You've gone off in different directions. I think you need your own space. Do you two *have* to share a room?"

"No," Carolyn answered, brightening.

"Then why doesn't one of you move into the guest room? Or the sewing room? There are plenty of rooms on this floor."

"Yeah!"

So Carolyn and I ran downstairs and interrupted Marilyn's practicing. We told her our idea.

"Yeah!" exclaimed Marilyn as happily as Carolyn had.

From then on, the afternoon was fun. The

116

twins talked and made plans. They giggled. They couldn't wait for their mother to come home. When she did, they greeted her at the back door with cries of "Mommy! Mommy!"

"What? What is it?" Mrs. Arnold looked slightly alarmed.

"Could we have our own rooms?" asked Marilyn.

"I want the guest room!" said Carolyn.

"I want the sewing room!" said Marilyn.

Mrs. Arnold looked questioningly at me. I shrugged. "The girls seem to be having a little trouble sharing their room," I said. "I just *mentioned* separate rooms, and . . ." I trailed off.

"Well," said Mrs. Arnold, "I don't see why not. But your room is so cute now," she told the twins.

"We're not babies anymore," said Carolyn. "And we're not the same person. We're different."

"But why do you want the sewing room?" Mrs. Arnold asked Marilyn. "It's so small."

"I just do," Marilyn replied. "I like it."

"And I like the guest room," said Carolyn. "Our old bedroom could be the guest room."

Mrs. Arnold's eyes began to gleam. "It would be fun to redecorate," she said. "New curtains, new rugs, new bedspreads."

"But can *we* choose our own things?" asked Marilyn. "*You* can decorate the guest room any way you like."

"That's a deal," said Mrs. Arnold.

The twins began jumping up and down. They even hugged each other.

I went home feeling that I had accomplished something important.

CHAPTER 13

Thursday

I sat for Marilyn and Carolyn today. Boy, does their mother move fast when you say the word "redecorate." It's only been a few weeks since Mary Anne's brilliant idea, and the girls are in their new rooms. Not only are they in their new rooms, but their rooms have already been decorated. The guest room hasn't - it's a jumble of stuff from the sewing room and the guest room-- but give Mrs. Arnold a few more days and I bet that will be done over, too.

Anyway, the girls seemed really happy, not at all the way we've been describing them in this notebook lately. So that was a relief. They showed off their new rooms eagerly, and then they even went over to the Braddocks' together.

"Hi, Stacey! Hi, Stacey!"

Marilyn and Carolyn greeted Stacey at the door as if they were old friends, which they weren't. True, Stacey does see a little more of them now that she lives in their neighborhood, but she hasn't baby-sat for them very often.

It turned out that the twins were just eager to show off their new rooms — and Stacey hadn't seen them yet. Mrs. Arnold hadn't even left when the girls began tugging at Stacey's hands, pulling her upstairs.

"Look at my room first!" cried Marilyn.

"No, mine!" said Carolyn.

"Mine's closer," Marilyn pointed out.

"Oh, all right."

At the head of the stairs was the sewing room. It *was* small, but it was bright and sunny and made a perfectly nice, if cramped, bedroom. All of Marilyn's furniture had been moved into it. "But we had to move some of my toys downstairs," she told Stacey. "I didn't mind. Look. New wallpaper and a new rug and a new bedspread. See how they match? Mommy let me pick out everything."

"All yellow," Stacey said. "Very nice." Personally, she thought it was just a little on the dull side, but she would never have said so.

"Now come see my room," cried Carolyn. So she and her sister and Stacey passed the girls' old room, turned a corner, and entered Carolyn's new room. Boy, was it different from Marilyn's. The rug was shaggy and blue. The bedspread was printed with cats, and two pillows in the shape of cats sat at the head of the bed. The wallpaper was blue-and-white striped, and the curtains and wastebasket matched the bedspread. The wastebasket came complete with pointy cat ears and a furry cat tail.

"Neat," said Stacey. "I didn't know you like cats."

"I didn't, either," replied Carolyn, "but I saw all this stuff and I knew it was what I wanted. Mommy wanted me to get pink-flowered *everything* — "

"And she wanted me to get blue-flowered everything — " added Marilyn.

" — but then she remembered that she'd told us we could choose whatever we wanted. Within reason," finished up Carolyn.

"I think you each did a very nice job," said Stacey. "A room should reflect your personality. I'm glad your mom let you make your own decisions."

"So are we," said the twins at the same time.

Stacey waited a moment. Then she said, "Well? Aren't you going to hook pinkies? You just said the same thing at the same time."

The girls laughed. "If we hooked pinkies every time we did that," Carolyn began, "we might as well just have our pinkies joined."

"Yeah. We're always saying the same things at the same time. That's because we're twins."

"Identical, but different," added Marilyn.

Funny, thought Stacey. The twins had changed so much. They'd been allowed to go their separate ways and now they had their own rooms and their own friends. Yet they seemed closer than ever. Was that what moving apart could do? Make you grow closer?

It was something to think about.

"So what do you want to do today?" asked Stacey.

"You brought your Kid-Kit, didn't you?" Carolyn asked.

"Yup."

"Oh, goody! Is there anything new in it?"

"Come on down and see."

The girls raced ahead of Stacey to the living room, and Stacey placed the Kid-Kit on the floor. Marilyn and Carolyn watched eagerly as she opened it.

"Okay," said Stacey, "in place of the Doctor

Doolittle books we have the Mrs. Piggle-Wiggle books. And we have a new pad of paper and three sheets of new stickers. *Plus* pastels instead of crayons. Have you ever made a picture with pastels? They're neat. You can blend the colors with your fingers."

"Like chalk?" asked Marilyn.

"Sort of."

Stacey opened the new box of pastels and let the girls peer inside.

"Ooh," said the twins as they gazed at the tidy row of colors.

"Try experimenting," suggested Stacey. "We can sit at the kitchen table."

So they did.

Halfway into her picture of a boat on the ocean, Marilyn said, "This is going to be for Daddy. No, for Mommy. I haven't given her a picture in awhile. No, wait. It'll be for both of them."

"Mine will be for both of them, too," said Carolyn, looking at her close-up picture of a butterfly and a ladybug.

Interesting, thought Stacey. No more, "Mommy will like *mine* better . . ." or, "Daddy always likes *my* . . ." That was a nice change.

"Hey," she said, "why don't you make frames for your pictures? They're so pretty I think they ought to be framed."

"How do you make frames?" asked Carolyn.

"Like this." Stacey showed the twins how to cut out frames from construction paper and glue them onto the pictures.

"Cool!" exclaimed Carolyn. Then she turned her picture over and wrote *To Mommy and Daddy — Love, Carolyn*. So Marilyn turned *hers* over and wrote, *To Mommy and Daddy — Love Marilyn*.

Stacey expected sparks to fly since Marilyn had copied Carolyn, but nothing happened. Each twin made and framed another picture. When they were done, Carolyn said, "I think I'll call Haley."

Marilyn watched wistfully as her sister made the phone call.

"Come over?" Carolyn repeated into the receiver. "Sure. Let me ask Stacey first." Carolyn put her hand over the receiver and said, "Haley invited me over. Can I go? Claudia is baby-sitting there."

"Sure," said Stacey.

Then, to everyone's surprise, Carolyn said, "Marilyn, do you want to come, too?"

Marilyn's eyes widened. "Yeah!"

"Okay," said Carolyn.

"Wait a sec," Stacey broke in. "I better talk to Claud."

So Stacey and Claud had a conversation, and Claud said she didn't mind a bit if Stacey brought the twins over. "As long as they're not fighting," she added.

"No, no. Everything's fine," Stacey assured her. She put the Kid-Kit away, left a note for Mrs. Arnold, and she and the girls walked over to the Braddocks' house. It was a beautiful day and when they arrived, Stacey and Claud sat on the back deck and listened to the girls below them. Aside from the twins and Haley were Vanessa Pike and Charlotte Johanssen. Matt was playing at the Pikes'.

"You know," Stacey heard Haley say, "we should start our club. Right now. There are five of us. That's enough for a club."

"You want *me* in your club?" squeaked Marilyn.

The other girls looked at each other. Finally Carolyn said, "*Only* if you won't be too bossy. We'll try you for three meetings. If you're too bossy, you're out. Okay?"

"I guess."

Poor Marilyn, thought Stacey. She was on probation, but at least she'd been asked to join the club.

"What about your friend Gazelle?" asked Vanessa. "Do you think she'd want to join?"

"You mean Gozzie?" replied Marilyn. "Oh . . . oh, I don't know. I mean, I don't think so. She, um, she doesn't like clubs."

"Okay," said Vanessa, shrugging.

Stacey looked at Claudia. "You know what?" she said quietly. "I bet Gozzie Kunka is an imaginary friend of Marilyn's. I think Marilyn made her up because she didn't have any friends."

"Oh! I bet you're right!" exclaimed Claud. "I wonder if Gozzie will disappear now."

"I doubt it," replied Stacey. "At least not until Marilyn's club probation is over and she can be sure she'll have real friends."

Stacey and Claudia smiled at each other. And that night, Stacey called to tell me the news.

"You mean Gozzie Kunka is imaginary?" I cried. "I should have known. I just should have known. A foreign dignitary's daughter named Gozzie Kunka living in Stoneybrook. How could I have been so naive?"

I couldn't help laughing. It was pretty funny.

CHAPTER 14

Less than one week left until the wedding! I couldn't believe it. We'd made most of our plans, but there were still plenty of things to do.

"Imagine if we'd had the *huge* wedding we wanted," I said to Dawn in school on Monday. Since I'd had time to calm down about moving into her house, we were friends again. For one thing, Dad and Mrs. Schafer had *both* said that they would get rid of some of their furniture and combine the rest of it in Dawn's house.

"What will we do with the leftover stuff?" I'd asked.

"Store some of it in the barn," Dad had answered, "and probably give some to the Salvation Army."

For another thing, I had actually *seen* Mrs. Schafer pat Tigger. So I felt a lot better about the cat business.

For a third thing, I'd decided that I did want to redecorate my room at Dawn's (but keep most of my old furniture), and Claudia had said she would help me. She had helped Stacey redecorate when Stacey moved back to Stoneybrook. She's good at that sort of thing.

Anyway, to get back to that Monday in school, Dawn replied, "I know. If we'd really wanted to do all those things, it would have taken about a year to plan for the wedding."

"Yeah. Caterers, flower arrangers . . ."

"And dressmakers, tux rentals . . ."

We were becoming wedding experts.

"At least we're going to get new dresses after all," I said. The two of us had just joined the other BSC members at our usual table in the cafeteria. "You almost ruined that by taking back everything we'd said we wanted."

Dawn giggled. She opened her lunch bag and pulled out a package of carrot sticks and a container of salad that definitely had tofu in it.

"Ew, ew. Gross! Health food!" cried Kristy, holding her nose.

Dawn looked over at the school lunch Kristy had bought. "I will never," she said, pointing to Kristy's Jell-O, "understand how people can eat something that jiggles."

"Tofu jiggles," said Kristy.

"It does not. It's solid." To prove her point, Dawn poked her salad container. Nothing happened. Then she poked Kristy's plate. The Jell-O was practically dancing. And the six of us (Kristy, Dawn, Stacey, Claudia, Logan, and I) were hysterical.

"So what about your dresses?" Claudia said to Dawn and me. (Leave it to Claud to turn the discussion back to fashion.)

"We're each getting a new one," I replied.

"But not matching ones," added Dawn, "since we aren't going to be bridesmaids. We'll just be sitting in the chapel with you guys."

"And," said Dawn, "Mom picked out a beautiful pale pink dress with this beaded design all over it. It has a drop waist. It looks sort of old-fashioned — like something from the nineteen-twenties."

"Neat," said Claud.

"And if you can believe it," I spoke up, "Dawn's mom talked my dad into buying a new suit *and* new shoes. Dressy ones, I mean. I don't remember the last time he bought a new suit or new shoes."

There was a pause. Kristy poked at her Jell-O. "Well, now I can't eat this!" she cried.

"Why'd you have to say it jiggles?" she asked Dawn.

Dawn gave her a wry smile.

"So when's the big move?" Logan asked carefully.

Dawn and I glanced at each other. We both knew the subject was still touchy. I was reconciled to the move, but I hadn't forgiven Dad for not telling me about it earlier, or Dawn for just assuming I'd be delighted to move into her old house.

"It's sort of ongoing," I replied. "No 'big move.' Dad has already put some of our stuff in Dawn's barn."

"Mom's put some things in there, too," said Dawn, "and had the Salvation Army pick up some other things."

"And we'll move the rest of our furniture and cartons over on the day after the wedding, when our parents get back from the Strathmoore Inn," I added. "What a day that will be. My father will want everything put away and organized immediately, and Dawn's mom — "

" — could let the stuff sit there for months," Dawn finished.

Logan squeezed my hand. "If I can help

with the move, just let me know," he said softly.

Dawn and I walked partway home from school together that day.

"You know what we've never talked about?" she said. "I mean, what you and I and our parents have never talked about?"

"What?" I asked.

"What we'll call our stepparents. I still call your father Mr. Spier and you still call my mother Mrs. Schafer."

"I guess we could call them by their first names," I said, "but I'd feel really funny calling your mom Sharon."

"And I'd feel funny calling your dad Richard."

"We could call them Mommy and Daddy," I suggested, giggling.

"No, Stepmother and Stepfather!" said Dawn. "That would make everyone feel *really* comfortable."

"How about Gertrude and Horace?" I said.

Dawn laughed so hard she started to cry. "Mary Anne," she said, "when we're not fighting, we have so much fun together. Don't you think we should share my room after all?

We could stay up late at night and talk with the lights out. We could share secrets. We could do our homework together. Isn't that what sisters do? I've always wanted a sister."

"Me, too," I confessed.

"So why *don't* we share my room? The guest room can stay the guest room and you can put your bed and desk in my room. It'll be a little crowded, but not too bad."

I was beginning to feel excited. "Would you mind having Tigger in the room at night? He always sleeps with me."

"No, I'd love it! Do you think he'd sleep with me sometimes?"

"Maybe. He's a sucker for a warm body. He'll wrap himself around your head and purr in your ear."

"Hey! We can share clothes!" exclaimed Dawn enthusiastically. "We're almost the same size. I'm just taller than you. Our wardrobe will double."

"Oh, speaking of wardrobes, I've been thinking," I said. "Our parents may not be having a big traditional wedding, but I do think that your mom at least ought to wear something old, something new, something borrowed, and something blue on the wedding day. Like in that old saying. Don't you?"

Dawn nodded. "Definitely. Well, let's see. Her brooch is old — it's an antique — she's borrowing a necklace from her mother, I think her earrings are sapphires, but . . . something new, hmm. I wonder if her dress counts. Most brides have new dresses. I'll talk to her, okay?"

"Okay."

The next afternoon, Mrs. Schafer (oh, excuse me, Sharon) took Dawn and me shopping for our new dresses. We went to Bellair's Department Store first, where I found a pink dress that I only halfway liked, and Dawn didn't find anything. So we left and went to Talbots, but we didn't find anything there, either.

"How about Zingy's, that new store?" suggested Dawn.

Sharon took one step inside Zingy's and backed out, pulling us with her. "No way, young lady," she said to Dawn. "This place is pure punk."

Finally we went to the mall and tried the Laura Ashley store. There Dawn found a sort of hip sailor dress. "I can wear my ankle boots with this," she said.

So Dawn was set. I looked at the more feminine clothes, but couldn't find a thing. Then it occurred to me — what I really wanted to wear was Dawn's other Laura Ashley dress, the one she'd worn to her mother's surprise supper.

"Hey, roomie," I said, "can I wear the flowered dress you got here for your mom's party?"

"Sure, roomie!" she replied. And then she added, "See how much fun we're going to have when you move in?"

I grinned. I did see. I really did.

On Thursday night, Jeff came in from California. Dad, Dawn, her mother, the Pike triplets — Byron, Jordan, and Adam — and I met him at the airport. The triplets were going to be Jeff's guests at the wedding. He had phoned them from California to invite them. (I might add here that all the inviting had been done over the phone, which I thought was just awful. It seemed to me that the least Dad and Mrs. Sch — I mean, Sharon, could have done was mail out invitations. They didn't have to be engraved or anything.)

The seven of us met Jeff at the airport at eight-thirty. We were carrying a sign that said

WELCOME HOME, JEFF. I would have died if anyone had met me with a big, personal sign at an airport, but everyone said Jeff would love it, and they were right. For one thing, he spotted us right away and didn't have to worry that he wouldn't find us. For another thing, he loved the attention.

"Hi! Hi, everybody!" he called.

We surrounded Jeff, all laughing, hugging, and talking at the same time. Jeff showed us the stuff he'd collected on the plane — salt and pepper packets from his meal, a plastic fork, a free magazine, and a bar of soap from the bathroom, which he presented to his mother with great fanfare.

"Well, how does it feel to be back on the East Coast?" my father asked Jeff as we were walking out to the Pikes' station wagon, which we'd had to borrow in order to take so many people to the airport.

"Just fine, sir," Jeff replied, and I realized that my father and Jeff barely knew each other.

"You can call me Richard," Dad said immediately, and then added, "or whatever feels the most comfortable."

"Okay, sir," said Jeff. Then he ran ahead to catch up with the triplets.

Dad looked at Sharon, bewildered, and she said, "It'll work out. We just have to give it some time."

Dad nodded.

I felt sorry for him.

The next night, the night before the wedding, the future Spier-Schafer family had a quiet dinner at Dawn's house. Jeff was still acting pleasant but ever so polite and formal around Dad, saying, "Yes, sir," and "No, sir." That was the only thing he called him. He also mentioned that he and his dad often went to sporting events in California.

Dad cringed. I don't think he has ever been to a major sporting event.

Then Jeff accidentally dropped the name Carol, and it turned out that his father has a girlfriend. Sharon cringed then, but we got over that hump and had a very nice dinner. I looked around the table — Dad, Sharon, Dawn, Jeff, and me. This was my new family. I decided I liked it. And I even admitted to myself that I'd always liked Dawn's rambling old farmhouse.

When dinner was over, Dawn and I watched some TV with Jeff. Then we went upstairs to Dawn's room.

"See?" she said to me. "Your bed can go right there. And your desk can go next to mine. We'll do our homework together every night. It'll be kind of like study hall."

"And I'll just squeeze all my clothes into your closet. That way we can share everything," I said.

Dawn held her hand out and we slapped five. "Sisters?" she said.

"Sisters," I replied.

CHAPTER 15

I'd been pretty excited on Friday night by the time Dad and I got home. But that was nothing compared to the excitement I felt when I woke up on Saturday morning.

It was wedding day!

By that evening I would have an official stepmother, stepsister, and stepbrother. Dad and I would never be lonely again. We would never be facing the world alone together again.

So why didn't that thought comfort me? I felt unsettled. Dad and I had done pretty well facing the world alone. Did I really want that to change? Then I thought of sharing a room with Dawn and being able to discuss girl problems with Sharon. I decided I could handle the change.

"Mary Anne!" I heard my father call. I was still in bed, thinking over what the day was going to bring.

"Coming!" I replied.

The wedding was to be held at noon in the chapel of our church. Afterward, everyone at the wedding would go out to lunch. And we *were* going to Chez Maurice, since that was where Dad had given Sharon the engagement ring. The maitre d' had reserved a table for twenty in a private room for us. I couldn't wait to see what a table for twenty would look like.

I spent most of the morning just getting dressed. I called Dawn six times for advice and finally asked Claudia to come over and help me. Claudia brought her makeup. I thought Dad would have a fit, but Claud said she could make me up so you'd never know I had makeup on. I'd just look pretty and natural. She also decided to do something spectacular to my hair, involving French braids.

By eleven o'clock I was ready. If I do say so myself, I looked *good*. Dawn's dress fit me perfectly, although it was longer on me than it had been on her. Claudia had put *very* pale gloss on my lips, more clear polish on my nails, light mascara on my lashes, extremely pale blue shadow on my eyelids, and just a hint of rouge on my cheeks. Then she had expertly braided my hair. I felt a little bad that Dawn didn't have Claudia's help, but then she had a mother — and soon I would, too.

By the time Claudia left, Dad was also dressed. He looked quite natty (his word) in his new shoes and gray suit. He came into my room to see how I looked.

"Lovely," he said softly. "Beautiful. So grown-up. I can't believe how pretty you are. I'm sure Claudia will end up in fashion design or makeup artistry."

I shook my head, smiling. "Nope. She's going to be an artist."

"Mary Anne?" said Dad. "Come sit next to me on the bed."

"Okay," I replied. When I sat down I realized that Dad was holding a box in his hand.

"This is for you," he said. "Open it."

I did so. Inside lay a pearl necklace. "For me?!" I couldn't help exclaiming.

"Yes," said Dad. "It belonged to your mother. I was going to give it to you on your sixteenth birthday, but somehow, I think today is more appropriate. Do you want me to fasten it on for you?"

"Yes, please," I said, trying not to cry.

When Dad was finished, I looked at myself in the full-length bathroom mirror. I could hardly believe that the person reflected there was me. I *did* look grown-up and beautiful, especially with my mother's necklace.

"Well," said Dad. "Are you ready to leave? The minister asked Sharon and me to arrive a little early. He wants to go over parts of the ceremony with us beforehand."

"I'm ready," I said. I kissed Tigger good-bye, and Dad and I left for the church.

We arrived just as the Schafers did, which was a miracle because Sharon is usually late. Dawn must have been prodding her all morning. As soon as they got out of their car, I knew I was right. Dawn *had* been prodding her. If she hadn't, Sharon would have turned up with a run in her stockings or nonmatching earrings, or the tag at the back of her dress would have been sticking out. But she looked perfect.

And Dawn was gorgeous in her new dress, while Jeff looked handsome but uncomfortable in what was probably a new suit.

"Hi!" we called as we piled out of our cars.

Dad and Sharon hugged.

Then Dawn and I hugged, and she squealed, "Who did your hair?"

Jeff stood back, looking more uncomfortable than ever.

Half an hour later, the service began. Dawn, Jeff, their grandparents, and I got to sit in the very first pew. Right behind us were Kristy, Logan, Jessi, Dawn, Stacey, and Claud. Behind them were Dad and Sharon's friends from work, and several rows behind *them*, in a pew all to themselves, were the triplets, as dressed up as Jeff, but appearing slightly mischievous. I hoped they weren't going to do anything to ruin the ceremony.

The chapel looked very nice. I mean, it's pretty to begin with, but Dawn's grandparents had sent two huge bouquets of flowers to the church, which had been placed on either side of the altar. The flowers were pink and white, so Dawn and I had *both* gotten our ways.

We sat quietly in the chapel. After awhile the organ began to play. Then my dad and Dawn's mom appeared at the back of the church. Sharon was carrying a bouquet of roses and baby's breath. Everyone turned around to look at them and watch them walk slowly up the aisle. (Sharon didn't want her father to "give her away." She didn't like the idea of *being* "given away" in the first place, as if she were something someone owned, and also she and Dad wanted to keep the service as simple as possible.)

Dad and Sharon had walked about three steps when I began to cry. Everything was just so . . . beautiful and meaningful. I fingered my pearl necklace and the tears started falling faster.

Dawn nudged me. "I hope you have Kleenex," she whispered loudly.

I nodded. Of course I did. I'm never without them.

My father and Dawn's mother were about halfway up the aisle, when I noticed a commotion in the triplets' pew. They were pointing at something, trying to attract Jeff's attention, and turning red from holding in their laughter.

I scanned the chapel to see what could possibly be so funny. I hoped Dad didn't have a rip in his new pants. No, the triplets were pointing past Dad to a stained glass window with a picture of an angel coming down from heaven. So, okay, the angel was sort of scantily dressed, but you couldn't see a *thing*. I mean, every part of her that should have been covered up was covered up. But you know how it is when you're the triplets' age and you see something like that. I vowed to tell Mallory not to let the triplets go to an art museum until they were at least twenty, because of all the paintings and statues of naked people.

The triplets distracted me from crying for

about ten seconds. Then, Dad and Sharon reached the altar, stood before the minister, and I started all over again. At least I had the sense to get some Kleenex out of my purse. I dabbed at my eyes. The Kleenex turned *black*. Oh, no! The mascara was coming off. I turned to Dawn.

"Do I look like a raccoon?" I whispered.

"Yes," she replied.

I concentrated so hard on getting all the mascara off of my face that I missed most of the ceremony, short as it was. I didn't look up again until I heard the minister say, "I now pronounce you husband and wife. You may kiss the bride," he added to Dad.

Oh, my gosh. My *father* was going to *kiss Dawn's mother* in front of all these people? Oh, no. Oh, *no*. The triplets began snickering again. I couldn't look at Dad, so I pulled another piece of Kleenex (the last one) out of my purse, wiped at my eyes again (just for effect), and proceeded to rub all the blue eyeshadow off.

"Good going," said Claud from behind me. She could see the blue Kleenex.

Oh, well. There was nothing I could do about the way I looked. I just watched Dad and Sharon walk happily down the aisle. They were married! I could scarcely believe it. My new family was real now.

Dinner at Chez Maurice (well, it was called dinner, but it was really lunch) started out fine. I loved our private room and our long table with the guests seated up and down each side.

As soon as we had given the waiter our orders, I leaned over to Dawn and whispered, "Did your mom ever find something new to wear today?"

"Yup," she replied, giggling. "She got new underwear."

Then we began talking about that night. While our parents went to the Strathmoore Inn, Jeff was going to stay at the Pikes' (they'd barely notice another kid), and Dawn and I were going to spend the night alone at my house. My room was half packed up, but I wanted one last night there.

My friends and I talked, drank soda, ate bread sticks, and waited for the food to arrive. When it did, I watched Dad offer Sharon a bite of his veal roast, but Sharon turned it down and Dad looked slightly hurt. Then I checked out everyone else's dinners, since Dawn and Jeff had been complaining because there weren't enough vegetarian dishes on the menu. I told myself not to start feeling crabby and spoil the celebration.

But at that moment, I heard Sharon say something about, ". . . dirty litter box to clean out every day."

Humphh. For her information, Tigger rarely uses the litter box. His idea of "outdoors" is that it's one big bathroom. When he does use his box, I clean it myself.

I sat there feeling crabby after all. I thought of the Schafers' messy house. I thought of my room and how much I would miss it. I had just worked myself into a real crab condition when Dawn surprised me by handing me a box and saying, "This is a 'now-we're-sisters' present."

Inside was a beautiful silver barrette.

I should have been grateful, but I felt even worse because of course I hadn't thought to get Dawn a "now-we're-sisters" present.

"Thank you, D — " I started to say, but just then, Sharon stood up.

"It's time for the throwing of the bouquet!" she announced. "All unmarried women — or girls — gather in that corner of the room," she said, pointing. "The one who catches the bouquet will be the next bride."

There was a rush for the corner. Everyone

pushed and shoved. Dawn and I managed to make our way to the front of the crowd.

Mrs. Schafer stood on her chair. She turned her back and tossed the bouquet over her shoulder. It was heading straight for Dawn and me. We both jumped for it.

To be continued in book #31. . . .

About the Author

ANN M. MARTIN did *a lot* of baby-sitting when
she was growing up in Princeton, New Jersey.
Now her favorite baby-sitting charge is her cat,
Mouse, who lives with her in her Manhattan
apartment.

Ann Martin's Apple Paperbacks are *Bummer
Summer, Inside Out, Stage Fright, Me and Katie
(the Pest)*, and all the other books in the Baby-
sitters Club series.

She is a former editor of books for children,
and was graduated from Smith College. She
likes ice cream, the beach, and *I Love Lucy*; and
she hates to cook.

Look for #31

DAWN'S WICKED STEPSISTER

I don't know about Mary Anne, but suddenly I realized just how loud our fighting had become. And wouldn't you know, about three seconds later Mom and Richard ran into our room.

"All right," said Richard, "what's going on in here?"

He and Mom were standing just inside the doorway, looking from me to Mary Anne and back again. They were waiting for an answer.

Mary Anne pointed at me. "*She* is being too noisy," she told her father. "I can't concentrate on my homework."

I pointed at Mary Anne. "*She* wants total silence," I told my mother. "*I* can't concentrate on *my* homework that way."

"The easy solution to this," said Richard, "is for you to do your homework in separate rooms."

"But who's going to leave?" asked Mom. She put her hands on Mary Anne's shoulders. Mary Anne just kept on crying.

"You know," I said to Mary Anne, "when my *real* brother was living here, we hardly ever fought like this. In fact, you and I didn't fight until you moved in."

"Until we became *step*sisters," said Mary Anne angrily.

"Okay, okay, that's enough," said Richard. "Do you girls think you can work this problem out tonight?"

"Yes," I said. "I'll work in the stupid guest room."

"Don't bother," replied Mary Anne. "It would be silly for you to do that since I'm going to be sleeping there tonight." And with that, she started yanking the covers off of her bed.

Mom gave me a look that plainly said, "*Now* see what you've done?"

But I didn't care. Mary Anne was just as much a part of this problem as I was. If she wanted to go and sleep in the guest room — fine. That was her decision. She sure was making me look bad, though. I had not, I realized, gotten just a stepsister. I'd gotten a wicked stepsister.

Read all the books
in the Baby-sitters Club series
by Ann M. Martin

#1 *Kristy's Great Idea*
Kristy's great idea is to start *The Baby-sitters Club*!

2 *Claudia and the Phantom Phone Calls*
Someone mysterious is calling Claudia!

3 *The Truth About Stacey*
Stacey's different . . . and it's harder on her than anyone knows.

4 *Mary Anne Saves the Day*
Mary Anne is tired of being treated like a baby. It's time to take charge!

5 *Dawn and the Impossible Three*
Dawn thought she'd be baby-sitting — not *monster*-sitting!

6 *Kristy's Big Day*
Kristy's a baby-sitter — and a bridesmaid, too!

7 *Claudia and Mean Janine*
Claudia's big sister is super smart . . . and super *mean*.

8 *Boy-Crazy Stacey*
Stacey's too busy being *boy-crazy* to baby-sit!

9 *The Ghost at Dawn's House*
Creaking stairs, a secret passage — there must be a ghost at Dawn's house!

#10 *Logan Likes Mary Anne!*
Mary Anne has a crush on a *boy* baby-sitter!

#11 *Kristy and the Snobs*
The kids in Kristy's new neighborhood are S-N-O-B-S!

#12 *Claudia and the New Girl*
Claudia might give up the club — and it's all Ashley's fault!

#13 *Good-bye Stacey, Good-bye*
Oh, no! Stacey McGill is moving back to New York!

#14 *Hello, Mallory*
Is Mallory Pike good enough to join the club?

#15 *Little Miss Stoneybrook . . . and Dawn*
Everyone in Stoneybrook has gone beauty-pageant crazy!

#16 *Jessi's Secret Language*
Jessi's new charge is teaching her a *secret language.*

#17 *Mary Anne's Bad-Luck Mystery*
Will Mary Anne's bad luck ever go away?

#18 *Stacey's Mistake*
Has Stacey made a big mistake by inviting the Baby-sitters to New York City?

#19 *Claudia and the Bad Joke*
Claudia is headed for trouble when she baby-sits for a practical joker.

152

#20 *Kristy and the Walking Disaster*
Can Kristy's Krushers beat Bart's Bashers?

#21 *Mallory and the Trouble with Twins*
Sitting for the Arnold twins is double trouble!

#22 *Jessi Ramsey, Pet-sitter*
Jessi has to baby-sit for a house full of . . . *pets!*

#23 *Dawn on the Coast*
Could Dawn be a California girl for good?

#24 *Kristy and the Mother's Day Surprise*
There are all *kinds* of surprises this Mother's Day.

#25 *Mary Anne and the Search for Tigger*
Tigger is missing! Has he been catnapped?

#26 *Claudia and the Sad Good-bye*
Claudia never thought she'd have to say good-bye
to her grandmother.

#27 *Jessi and the Superbrat*
Jessi gets to baby-sit for a TV star!

#28 *Welcome Back, Stacey!*
Stacey's moving again . . . back to Stoneybrook!

#29 *Mallory and the Mystery Diary*
Only Mal can solve the mystery in the old diary.

#30 *Mary Anne and the Great Romance*
Mary Anne's father and Dawn's mother are getting
married!

#31 *Dawn's Wicked Stepsister*
Dawn thought having a stepsister was going to be
fun. Was she ever wrong!

153

Super Specials:

1 *Baby-sitters on Board!*
Guess who's going on a dream vacation? The Baby-sitters!

2 *Baby-sitters' Summer Vacation*
Good-bye Stoneybrook . . . hello Camp Mohawk!

3 *Baby-sitters' Winter Vacation*
The Baby-sitters are off for a week of winter fun!

America's Favorite Series

THE BABY-SITTERS Club®

by Ann M. Martin

Collect Them All!

The seven girls at Stoneybrook Middle School get into all kinds of adventures...with school, boys, and, of course, baby-sitting!

☐ MG41588-3	Baby-sitters on Board! Super Special #1	$2.95
☐ MG41583-2	#19 Claudia and the Bad Joke	$2.75
☐ MG42004-6	#20 Kristy and the Walking Disaster	$2.75
☐ MG42005-4	#21 Mallory and the Trouble with Twins	$2.75
☐ MG42006-2	#22 Jessi Ramsey, Pet-sitter	$2.75
☐ MG42007-0	#23 Dawn on the Coast	$2.75
☐ MG42002-X	#24 Kristy and the Mother's Day Surprise	$2.75
☐ MG42003-8	#25 Mary Anne and the Search for Tigger	$2.75
☐ MG42419-X	Baby-sitters' Summer Vacation Super Special #2	$2.95
☐ MG42503-X	#26 Claudia and the Sad Good-bye	$2.95
☐ MG42502-1	#27 Jessi and the Superbrat	$2.95
☐ MG42501-3	#28 Welcome Back, Stacey!	$2.95
☐ MG42500-5	#29 Mallory and the Mystery Diary	$2.95
☐ MG42499-8	Baby-sitters' Winter Vacation Super Special #3	$2.95
☐ MG42498-X	#30 Mary Anne and the Great Romance	$2.95
☐ MG42497-1	#31 Dawn's Wicked Stepsister (February '90)	$2.95
☐ MG42496-3	#32 Kristy and the Secret of Susan (March '90)	$2.95
☐ MG42495-5	#33 Claudia and the Mystery of Stoneybrook (April '90)	$2.95
☐ MG42494-7	#34 Mary Anne and Too Many Boys (May '90)	$2.95
☐ MG42508-0	#35 Stacey and the New Kids on the Block (June '90)	$2.95

For a complete listing of all the Baby-sitter Club titles write to :
Customer Service at the address below.
Available wherever you buy books...or use the coupon below.

Scholastic Inc. P.O. Box 7502, 2932 E. McCarty Street, Jefferson City, MO 65102

Please send me the books I have checked above. I am enclosing $_____
(please add $2.00 to cover shipping and handling). Send check or money order–no cash or C.O.D.'s please.

Name_____

Address_____

City_____ State/Zip_____

Please allow four to six weeks for delivery. Offer good in U.S.A. only. Sorry, mail order not available to residents of
Canada. Prices subject to change. BSC 789